BENJAMIN'S BRIDE

SEVEN BRIDES FOR SEVEN BROTHERS
BOOK SEVEN

KATHLEEN LAWLESS

Seven Brides for Seven Brothers Reviews

What reviewers are saying about the *Seven Brides for Seven Brothers* series...

"GREAT SERIES!!!" Top 500 reviewer

"If you have not picked up the series, do yourself a favor, you will be glad you do."

"I loved the continuity in the series—and the resolution"

"Sweet and romantic."

"This entire series is going into my library to be read again and again."

"I just love reading Kathleen's books—they keep me coming back for more."

If you haven't already done so, sign up for my VIP Reader's Newsletter and be the first to hear about free books, fan-priced sales, and my new series. Details at the end of the book.

Dedication

To my three amazing children who have always supported my writing.

CHAPTER 1

Georgina watched Amanda, seated at the fancy grand piano that had been imported for the newly built Grande Hotel, signal to where Lily waited at the top of the hotel lobby's sweeping staircase. The air was faintly tinged with a delicate floral scent wafting from the decorated archway at the entrance to the hotel. At Lily's nod, the familiar notes of the wedding march swirled through the air.

Rose, Lily's sister and matron of honor, in a shimmering blue gown, started down the massive curved stairway first. After a slight delay Lily followed, one hand gripping her bouquet of lilies, the other hand holding tight to the banister. With her blonde hair piled high in ringlets, Lily looked like a fairy princess in a simple white gown made from the smoothest silk and trimmed with French lace at the cuffs and throat.

Georgina dabbed the moisture from her eyes, heaved a sigh, and tucked her hankie back into her reticule. She was happy for Lily—for the couple who had started off fighting like cats and dogs and eventually learned they couldn't live without each other.

Georgina's melancholy came from knowing this was the last Mason wedding she would be here for. No one knew yet of her plans to sell the café and move to Seattle and she didn't want her news to take away from the newlyweds' special day.

In spite of herself, her gaze drifted past the line of black-suited Mason brothers to rest on Benjamin, as it always did, and her heart gave a sad little flutter. He looked so handsome in his dark suit which matched the others groomsmen, even though he somehow held himself apart. Perhaps because he stood farthest from the groom.

Georgina had no doubt Benjamin would miss her for a short while. But she could no longer keep up the pretense that her interest stemmed from friendship alone as she listened to his hopes and fears, his dreams and doubts, his innermost thoughts, hanging on his every word.

To stay would mean she'd have to pretend she was happy for him when his turn came to marry. Pretending to be happy would be impossible—given that a little piece broke off her heart every time she saw him, knowing he would never look at her the way Barron was looking at Lily right this minute. It was for the best that she move away. Start over fresh.

She pulled her attention from Benjamin back to the happy couple as they exchanged rings and shared their first kiss as newlyweds. As soon as the formalities were over and the registry was signed, Georgina found her way to the hotel's large and modern kitchen at the rear of the building to check on the wedding feast. Her café was closed for the day, the staff all here at the hotel bustling about, ensuring the food preparation and set up went smoothly.

No one paid her any mind as the café's cook pulled a massive roasted haunch of beef from the oven, then turned to issue orders to the others. She stepped back, clearly in the way. Not needed here or anyplace else.

A handful of guests mingled in the lobby, checking out the building's architectural details. The hotel had officially opened its doors today, just in time for the wedding. With no guests registered yet, Henrietta had thrown open all the guest rooms, encouraging everyone there for the wedding to explore this newest addition to their town. Georgina had a preview earlier and knew that each room had been decorated to a different theme. Trust Henrietta to do things a notch above everyone else.

Georgina wandered over to the piano where Amanda sat playing a light background tune. "It's quite something," Georgina said as she trailed one hand along the piano's highly polished surface, where she could see her own reflection.

Amanda smiled up at her. "The piano? Or the hotel?"

"Both are definitely in a class of their own." Georgina worried her lower lip. "Does it bother you at all? Seeing the hotel here on the site of your mother's house where you grew up?"

Amanda shook her glossy head. "The ranch is home now for myself and my family. The town needs the hotel to attract visitors to this part of the territory."

Before she could ask why that was, they were joined by Amanda's husband, Bradley, holding the couple's young son who was red-faced and squirming in his father's arms.

"Sam's tired of his pa," Bradley said, tightening his grip.

"I'll take him." Georgina reached for the wiggly little guy. "Why don't you two go have a look around?"

"You don't mind?" Amanda rose from the piano bench,

clearly delighted to have a few minutes alone with her husband.

"Not at all." The youngster immediately grasped the buttons fronting her dress with his chubby fingers as she settled him onto one hip. "Things are well under control in the kitchen and I'm feeling quite at loose ends."

"Come on." Amanda grabbed Bradley's arm and danced away. "Let's go mess up one of the guest rooms."

Georgina blushed and looked down at the youngster in her arms. "Maybe you'll have a baby brother or sister before the year is out."

"Who'll be having a brother or sister?"

Georgina started. How had she been unaware of Benjamin's approach? Usually her inner senses warned her when he was nearby.

Benjamin offered a finger to baby Samuel, who grasped hold and grinned a toothless grin. "Sure does look like his pa."

"Yes," Georgina said. "They need a little red-headed girl to take after her mother. In fact, they may be working on that right now, upstairs."

Benjamin barked out a laugh. "I have to say, Amanda is for sure the best thing that ever happened to old Bradley."

Georgina swallowed thickly. One day someone would say the same about Benjamin and the woman who was lucky enough to claim his heart and become his bride.

To her surprise, Benjamin gave her a long, approving look. "Look at you," he said. "Packing the boy around as if you've been doing it all your life."

Georgina felt her face redden. It wasn't exactly a compliment but, coming from Benjamin, it was close. "He doesn't weigh any more than a load of dirty plates," she said. "He's just a little more wiggly is all."

She was relieved to see Benjamin's brother, Braydon, and his wife, Henrietta coming their way. Spending time with Benjamin as his friend was getting harder all the time.

"The hotel is amazing," she told Henrietta when the couple reached their side. "You did a great job."

"We both did." Henrietta smiled up at her husband, and he smiled back, an exchange so intimate it caused a lump in Georgina's throat.

Would that someone looked at *her* that way.

"It was a mad scramble to get everything finished for today," Henrietta added, "but it was worth it. I couldn't have managed it without the help of Braydon and the other brothers, including you, Ben."

"Happy to help," Benjamin said, staring at the ground as he spoke.

Georgina shot him a look. This was the first she had heard about Benjamin helping at the hotel. Maybe he didn't tell her everything the way she thought.

"I think my cook has fallen in love with the kitchen. I may never lure him back to the cafe," Georgina said.

Henrietta blanched. "I never thought ... Will I be taking business from you once the hotel is open and people are dining here?"

Georgina shook her head. "I expect the town will only get busier now that there's somewhere for visitors to stay. Folks'll be happy to have a choice of where to eat. I expect they're bored to tears with the same food we serve at the café every day."

Which was one more reason to move on and let the new owners put their mark on the place.

"There will definitely be enough business for both," Braydon said. "Lots of changes in the works around here, with plenty more to come."

Georgina nodded, aware she wouldn't be here to see them.

"It's hard to believe Hawkes managed to give every law man in the territory the slip," she said. "Is it possible he's still alive and made a successful escape?" She shuddered at the thought that she might inadvertently run into the evil-doer when she moved up north.

Braydon shook his head. "We got off so many shots when he dove into the pond, some of them had to hit him. I predict he crawled off to die and they'll find his body one of these days."

"Saves the territory the trouble of keeping him alive in jail," Benjamin added.

Georgina's gaze shifted from Benjamin to Braydon and back to Benjamin. Did the Mason brothers know something they weren't telling anyone else?

No sooner did the thought surface than they were joined by the one man who might have the answer—Marshal Philips, who was accompanied by a handsome older man Georgina had not seen around these parts before.

"I hope we're not interrupting, folks," Philips said. "Now that the ceremony is done with, I've got someone here who's anxious to meet the family, especially you, Braydon."

"If this is a family matter," Georgina said, "I can—"

"You're same as family to us," Benjamin said. His hand gripped her free arm, urging her to stay.

"Like a sister, you mean," Georgina said, swallowing the salty taste of sadness.

"That's right," Benjamin said. "Just like a sister."

"We need Brody and the others here for this," Philips said. "Doc, you can start to fill Braydon in. Georgina, would you mind helping me round up the others?"

"Not at all." Georgina thrust Samuel into the arms of a surprised Benjamin. "Here. You take him, please."

Benjamin's arms closed awkwardly around the youngster, "But I—"

Georgina ignored him to smile at Marshal Philips. "I believe we'll find the rest of the family this way."

Just before she walked away, Georgina saw Benjamin's speculative gaze pass from her to the marshal and back again, well aware Benjamin and the marshal had never seen eye to eye.

BENJAMIN WATCHED Georgina walk away with the marshal. He'd never liked the lawman, ever since the fella had first come sniffing around Bullet and suspected Braydon of stealing one of Henrietta's earrings. He glanced from the retreating couple to the boy in his arms, who was miraculously quiet and still.

The man who'd shown up with Philips cleared his throat. "Name's Doc Kennedy," he said. "Most folks call me Doc." He turned to Braydon. "I just found out recently that you're my nephew I never knew about. I'm Mary Quinn's brother."

Benjamin started. It wasn't long since Braydon had discovered the identity of his mother, along with a half-sister he never knew. Now, to have an uncle turn up out of the woodwork. Things were getting weirder all the time.

Braydon must have thought so as well. He said, "As I recall, when Paula was killed, Philips said something about the girl having relatives in high places. I take it that's you?"

Kennedy gave a rusty smile. "I've been helping out with some government stuff back in Tucson. Trying to figure some cohesive long-term plans for this territory along with a few of the others. Arizona may become a state one day soon."

Benjamin spoke up. "I've heard that talk. Lots of opposition to the idea." Kennedy shrugged. "Folks are never very welcoming to change. Not even me."

He cracked a half smile that set Benjamin's teeth on edge. It was a politician's smile if he ever saw one.

"I'm also not quite sure how I got roped into this gig in the first place. I knew Brody when he was still in short pants. Knew his pa as well, back in the day. Sat across a poker table from Brody more than once over the years."

"You're a gambler?" Benjamin said.

"Was," Kennedy said. "Turns out getting involved with the government was the biggest gamble I've ever taken." He laughed, and Braydon and Henrietta followed suit.

Benjamin just scowled.

"Here's Brody and the others now," Braydon said.

Benjamin looked up to see his other brothers and their wives approaching. Georgina brought up the rear with the marshal. The man walked so close to Georgina that his arm brushed hers. Which she didn't seem to mind a bit, as she looked up at the lawman with that intent look Benjamin knew well. It meant she was listening attentively to whatever the marshal was saying, her mouth curved in that beguiling half smile, her head tilted just so, the exact same way she did when she and Benjamin were deep in conversation. Her dark hair, pulled back in a tidy, yet attractive roll gleamed in the lamplight. Her features were dainty, and the color of her blue frock enhanced her eyes and her complexion.

"I'll take the baby now." Amanda stood before him, holding out her arms for her son. Benjamin had been staring so hard at Georgina and the marshal he hadn't even noticed her next to him.

"Ah, sure." He passed Samuel over. When he looked up again, Georgina was blocked from sight behind Brody.

"We should talk in the parlor," Brody said, indicating a room to the far side of the hotel's lobby.

Once everyone was inside, Philips closed the door and stood with his back to it. Benjamin scanned the group, but Georgina wasn't there.

"What happened to Georgina?" he asked Henrietta, who stood next to him.

"She said she didn't think it was appropriate that she be here," Henrietta responded, "for something that was obviously a family matter."

Benjamin pressed his lips together in frustration. Georgina was as much a part of this family as any of them.

"Listen up, everyone," Brody said. "You all know Marshal Philips. Some of you have met Doc Kennedy. For those who haven't, he's a big shot with the government these days. Also turns out he's Braydon's uncle. He's been helping us behind the scenes to get our hands on some of Hawkes's lending notes and we owe him a debt of thanks for that. Now that Hawkes is history, I'm not sure what he's doing here. But if I know Doc, we're about to find out."

"Thanks, Brody." Kennedy faced them with his hands clasped behind his back, obviously comfortable holding an audience.

"I figured it was high time I came out here and met this nephew of mine. But more than that. With Hawkes out of the way for good, it's time to make some serious plans as to where the lot of you would like to see this town of yours fit into the scheme of things. Taking over Hawkes's holdings makes you boys the biggest landowners in the area. Whatever happens next will affect you all the most."

"What do you think ought to happen?" Braydon asked.

Kennedy pursed his lips thoughtfully. "The way I see it, there are a few factors at play. Hawkes had a big mouth and word is already getting around about there being copper in the area. Wouldn't take much for things to get out of control and the area turn into a shanty town with a bunch of vagrants passing through looking to get rich quick. On the other hand, done right, you could see a controlled operation that hires decent folk and offers them a place to live. A reason to make Bullet their home and take pride in the town."

"Has there been any sign of Hawkes's men around the area?" Benjamin asked.

"Looks like everyone associated with him cleared out even before you boys staged that phony wedding. Problem is, we don't know where they are, how much they know, or who they're talking to," Kennedy said. "Which is why you need to devise a plan and start to put it in place. I have no doubt that if Hawkes had got hold of the ranch and started mining for copper, this entire territory would have been one lawless mess. Hawkes would have jacked up prices of everything, and not cared one whit about any folks who were interested in making an honest living."

"Do we have to open a copper mine?" Benjamin asked.

"I know that was not the wishes of Brody's uncle, rest his soul. But times change, like it or not. Copper is in demand. Brody and I have spoken several times on the topic."

Brody cleared his throat. "We can resist change, or we can implement change. Doc here has convinced me the latter is the best route for us, for Bullet, and for the future of our families. Not just those of us in this room, but for generations to come."

Doc nodded. "Smartest move is to be in the driver's seat." He turned to Brody. "One thing we haven't talked about yet is you running for mayor."

"Mayor?" Brody echoed.

"Yuma has itself a mayor. High time Bullet followed suit."

"What about the ranch? The mine when we get it started?"

"Strikes me as you're surrounded by a whole lot of capable helpers right here in this room. And another thing. Ever since Sheriff Yates was killed, there has been no lawman here to speak of. One job of the mayor would be to champion the man you want to uphold the law hereabouts. Someone you know you can trust."

Brody nodded. "Thanks, Doc. You've given us all a lot to think about. And now I believe we've kept the bride and groom away from their guests long enough. The bar's open. The food's almost ready. As one year ends and a new one begins, let's have ourselves a party!"

Benjamin hung back to talk to the twins. "Have either of you been keeping up the surveillance on Hawkes's place, just in case?"

Barron rolled his eyes. "I just got married. You think I've had any time to be ducking over to keep a look out?'

"Didn't strike me as there was any need," Bishop said.

Benjamin gave him a look. "And you're still on your honeymoon, right?"

Bishop gave him a cocky look. "Not officially. But it's never a bad idea to keep the pretense up. Try and make every day feel like a honeymoon."

"Lord help me," Benjamin said. "Am I the only one left who thinks being a bachelor is a good idea?"

"Kind of looks that way," Barron said.

"Don't you get lonely some of the time?" Bishop asked.

"Nah!" Benjamin shook his head. He had Georgina to look to when his own company got to be a little stale. "I hate to say it, but I'm starting to miss the old days."

"You heard Doc," Barron said. "These are the new days. Lots of changes ahead. Best decide how you'd like to see those changes come about so you're in charge, not simply along for the ride."

Uh-oh! Lily was bearing down on the three of them.

"Do you boys have to talk business on our wedding day?"

"It won't happen again, sweetheart," Barron said, slipping his arm around her waist. "I'm all yours. Let's go circulate."

Benjamin followed the trio into the hotel lobby, keeping an eye out for Georgina. By the time he spotted her over in the dining room supervising the laying out of the wedding feast, Marshal Philips stood next to her, chatting her up and doing a good job of it, judging by Georgina's laughter. He'd never heard her laugh like that with anyone other than him.

He was staring at the two of them so intently he didn't even notice Laura, his sister-in-law and Brody's wife, sidle up to him. "You could go join them you know."

Benjamin stiffened. "Why would I want to do that?"

Laura just gave him that knowing smile of hers. "I don't know, Ben. Why would you want to?"

"I don't want to," he said shortly. "Georgina's free to spend time with whomever she chooses."

"Strikes me there have been a lot of times lately when you were her first choice." Laura's gaze never left his.

"So?"

"Maybe she's tired of being taken for granted," Laura said. "Of being told she's like a sister."

"I don't—" He bit off his words. Hadn't he said that very thing just a few minutes earlier? "What's wrong with that?" he said defensively. "She has no other family since her ma passed."

"And now it's her turn. Strikes me as Georgina wants the same thing most women do. A home. A family. Someone to cherish her and make her feel special."

Benjamin glowered across the room. "Philips seems to be doing a mighty fine job of that right now." The man stood nose to toes to Georgina, his hand resting lightly on her arm as if it was his right to touch her.

Laura followed his gaze. "It's time someone did."

When Laura left to join Brody, Benjamin headed for the bar and a badly needed beer.

CHAPTER 2

Aware of Benjamin's glowering look from the far side of the hotel lobby, Georgina laughed a little louder than necessary at something the marshal said. Could the lawman be flirting with her? He was certainly touching her forearm a lot, bending close when he spoke, as if his words were for her alone.

"Thanks for your help earlier, Georgina, rounding up the Mason clan."

"I can tell you Lily wasn't pleased, having her wedding day taken over by business talk."

"Can't say I blame her for that. It was all Kennedy's doing. Speaking of the doc, I'd best go check on him, make sure he's behaving himself. Will you save me a spot to eat next to you?"

"What about Doc?" she asked. "Will he be joining us as well?"

"Heck no," Philips said. "Let Kennedy find his own pretty lady to sit next to."

Georgina smiled. Philips's compliment was a balm to her wounded pride, but the words would have sounded much sweeter coming from Benjamin, and nothing could change that.

"I would be honored to be your table mate for the meal." As she spoke, she slipped her hand into her pocket and felt the crinkled edges of the letter that had arrived the other day, offering her the job as cook at a logging camp near Seattle. She had yet to reply, but knew in her heart what her answer would be.

When the marshal left in search of Doc Kennedy, Georgina slowly circled the food table to ensure all was perfect, even though she knew her staff had served enough weddings lately that they had the routine down pat. She straightened a platter that didn't need straightening, and made sure the serving utensils were within easy reach.

She'd miss this—Bullet and the life she knew here. She'd also miss watching the new generations of Masons grow up. She could just picture the babies in a few years, old enough to run into the café for a scoop of the popular new ice cream she had started serving.

Finally satisfied all was ready, she signaled to Lily and Barron to lead the way to the table. After the bride and groom filled their plates with food and took their seats at the head table, the other guests lined up in an orderly fashion. She was waiting in line when Marshal Philips sought her out.

"How about I fix each of us a plate while you go snag us some seats?" He pointed to a table set for two near the far window. "Someplace quiet like that."

Georgina nodded and quickly moved across the hotel lobby to claim the table before anyone else got there. Her staff had worked quickly and efficiently to set the lobby, dining room and ballroom with tables, chairs and benches borrowed from all over town, enough to seat everyone for the wedding meal.

She took a seat and glanced about, admiring the special touches Henrietta had made to the hotel's interior, including a huge arrangement of fresh flowers on the mantle above a fireplace that was more for decoration than a heat source.

"Okay if I join you?" Benjamin stood before her holding a plate of food.

"I'm sorry," she said. "This seat is taken."

Benjamin frowned. "Usually you and I sit together at these affairs."

"Not this time," Georgina said.

Or any time in the future, because I won't be here.

She was saved from further comment by the arrival of the marshal.

"'Scuse me, lad." Philips slid past Benjamin and set a plate of food on the table in front of Georgina. "I hope I managed to pick out all your favorites."

Georgina smiled up at him. "You did very well. Thank you."

By the time the marshal took his seat across from her and unfolded his napkin, Benjamin was striding stiffly across the lobby. She watched out the window as he took his plate outside and sat with some of the local ranchers.

"Did Doc find someone to sit with?" Georgina asked, more to make conversation than real interest.

"He's with Brody and Laura. If Doc has his way, Bullet will soon elect Brody as its mayor."

"I wasn't aware of that plan," Georgina said. Nor would she be here to see it happen.

"Doc broached the subject earlier today," Philips said. "If

Bullet gets as busy as everyone expects it will, you'll do well with your café. Might even need to expand a second time."

"I'm afraid that's not going to happen," Georgina said. "I plan to sell in the new year, and I have someone interested in buying the place."

Philips looked up from his plate. "I hadn't heard that."

"No one knows yet," Georgina said. "I'd appreciate you keeping it to yourself until it's for sure. I was approached by a family from Mexico who are interested in moving here. They like the school for their children, and went back home to raise the capital they need."

Philips reached across the table and covered her free hand with his. "And where will that leave you? A lady of leisure?"

Georgina laughed. "Hardly. I have an opportunity up north."

"There are a lot of good opportunities out in Tucson if you planned to stay in the area. I know I would like that."

Georgina managed to slip her hand out from under his. "I'm very flattered, but my mind is already made up. It's time I saw other parts of the country besides Arizona."

"I understand."

The meal was followed by the speeches. Bishop told some amusing stories about his twin brother that had the guests laughing in delight. Georgina watched the front door, but didn't see Benjamin return. His place at the table with the other Masons remained conspicuously empty.

Outside, darkness slowly replaced the daylight as the tables were cleared and the room readied for dancing. The hotel glowed with cozy light from the gas lanterns Henrietta had had installed.

When a group of local musicians got out their instruments, Georgina wondered how long before she could slip away. Maybe she could make a discreet exit after Barron and Lily shared their first dance as a married couple. She planned to be gone long before Lily tossed her bouquet for the single ladies.

Across from her, Philips was chatting about something that failed to hold her interest, even though she must have smiled and nodded at the appropriate times. He was a pleasant enough man, just not the man who made her pulse race from nothing more than his presence.

Abruptly, from outside, the air was punctuated by a series of loud bangs. A quick glance out the window showed a cascade of sparks shooting high in the night sky.

Philips was on his feet, gun drawn and heading outside before Georgina left her chair. The Mason brothers were on Philips's heels, followed closely by their wives and Georgina quickly followed.

As the group burst out of the hotel, Henrietta, who was next to Georgina, let out a shriek of delight.

"Percy!" Henrietta raced toward the lone figure in the middle of the street who turned and made a familiar, theatrical bow toward the crowd.

"Happy New Year, everyone!"

His words were followed by a fresh volley of sounds that sounded like gunshots. A second blast of sparkly lights briefly illuminated the night sky before slowly disappearing from sight like snuffed-out stars. More guests crowded through the doorway and came outside as Henrietta threw herself into the arms of her old friend Percival Bloom.

Georgina had been planning to slip away quietly, but she was as curious as the rest of them to find out where Percy had been and what he had been up to.

"Trust old Percy to make an entrance like no one else." In the flare of the fireworks, Benjamin had spotted Georgina alone in the crowd and made his way to her side.

"Percy has always been larger than life," Georgina said. "What are those exploding lights?"

"He called them fireworks. Said they're the latest rage out in New York City and Boston for New Year's Eve festivities. Got me to help him set them up and get them ready." Benjamin let the pride ring through his words. Let Marshal Philips top that!

"Did you find out where Percy's been?"

"Sounds like all over," Benjamin said. He turned to Georgina, aware something had changed but hogtied if he knew what. He'd never had difficulty talking to her before. Quite the opposite: he found her a great listener. Oftentimes it felt like she knew what was on his mind even before he got out the words.

"Nice wedding," he said, as the silence between them lengthened.

"Lily and Barron seem very happy," Georgina said. "Quite a change from the way things started out between them."

Benjamin fell silent. Was Georgina thinking, as he was, how despite their initial animosity toward each other, Lily and Barron wound up finding true bliss together? Had that initial friction ultimately heightened the attraction?

There had never been any friction between him and Georgina. Quite the opposite. Any time he was with her felt as right, as comfortable, as anything ever had in his life. Here they were, in the middle of a hundred or more wedding guests, and it could have been just him and her alone. In fact, he wished it was just him and her. He didn't do crowds well.

He cleared his throat. "I guess we're all happy to see the end of Hawkes."

Georgina nodded, but she seemed distracted, not really listening to him the way she usually did.

"Shame you missed that chat earlier between Doc Kennedy and the family. He's trying to convince Brody to run for town mayor."

"Marshal Philips mentioned that over supper. It strikes me as a sound idea. Brody's uncle was one of the first settlers in the area, even before my parents."

"Yeah. Never really thought much about that. How you lived in the same place your entire life."

"Yes. Bullet has changed a lot from when I was a girl."

Benjamin tried to envision a young Georgina, but he couldn't. He'd bet she'd been one of those quiet, serious youngsters who always seemed older than their years. Probably had her nose stuffed in a book and her head in the clouds. Except he knew she'd worked at the café from the time she could toddle around and make herself useful.

He, too, hadn't had much of a childhood— growing up fast and hard because he'd had no other choice.

"You're lucky you had your ma in your life all these years."

"Yes. She slowed down some at the end, but she lived to see a good age."

She didn't say any more. She didn't have to.

Benjamin had confided to Georgina once how his mother had abandoned him after he shot the man who tried to rape her. What Georgina didn't know is that Hawkes had been one of the rapists. She also didn't know Ben had spent time in jail for killing his mother's other rapist before the authorities realized how young he was.

Ben wished he'd killed Hawkes that day as well. It would

have spared everyone he knew a lot of grief. But then he wouldn't have met Brody. Wouldn't have become part of this family, united by mutual hatred toward Hawkes, let alone been part of the takedown. And he never would have met Georgina. Her friendship meant everything to him.

After the fireworks ended, guests began to wander back inside. Benjamin heard the music start up and filter softly through the night air.

Suddenly he had the urge to put his arms around Georgina. To breathe deeply the familiar, soft fragrance of cooking spice he had come to associate with her. To feel her lips beneath his. He felt something other than comfortable familiarity standing here alongside her, fostering a sense of belonging that he had never experienced before this moment.

Georgina knew better than anyone else his deepest, darkest secrets, his less than stellar past, but she never judged.

Before he could turn to her and put his thoughts into action, she spoke. "It's getting late. I'll say good night."

She started to leave, away from him, away from the hotel.

"Don't go," he said.

She turned slowly and faced him. "How did you know what I was planning?"

He blinked rapidly, trying to make sense of her words. "Well, you said it was getting late."

"Yes. Yes, I did." Her voice sounded unaccountably sad. "Good night, Ben. And happy new year."

"Wait. I'll walk you home."

"You don't have to do that."

"Maybe I want to."

She waved a hand in the direction of the hotel behind

them, music and light spilling through the windows and out the open doorway. The night air felt velvety and mysterious. He smelled flowers.

"There are lots of young ladies inside hoping for a dance with you."

"I don't want to dance with them. Or with anyone else. Only you."

She let out a short, sharp laugh. "Don't tell me you're getting wedding-itis."

At his blank look, she continued. "It's been known to happen—especially at weddings. Suddenly anyone who is single feels they ought to hook up as well. Don't worry. By tomorrow the impulse will have faded. Things will be back to normal."

Ben shook his head. "It's not an impulse. It's like I suddenly woke up and saw you for the first time. I mean, really saw you."

She laid a soft hand against his cheek. "You're sweet, Ben. But earlier tonight you said you think of me as a sister."

"I was mistaken," he said stubbornly. "You mean a lot more to me than that. In fact, I think we ought to start spending time together."

"You and I have always spent time together."

"I don't mean like that. I mean, like romantic time together."

"I'm afraid that won't be possible," she said. "I was going to wait to tell you and the others."

"Tell us what?"

"That I'm moving to Seattle."

Ben felt like someone had clubbed him with a sledge hammer. His head swam. His ears rang. He couldn't focus.

"You can't be serious. This is your home. This is where you belong."

"I've been thinking about it for a while, ever since ma passed. She was too old to be moved, but with her gone, there's nothing keeping me here."

"What about the café?"

"I've had an offer from someone to purchase the café and the house."

BENJAMIN STARED AT HER WORDLESSLY, as if she'd suddenly grown two heads. That was a first, Georgina thought, Benjamin at a loss for words.

"I should go and say hello to Percy before I leave. Please excuse me." As she walked away, she could feel his eyes boring into her back. Inside the hotel, she found Percy near the wedding cake, talking to Henrietta.

"Am I interrupting?" she asked.

"Not at all," Henrietta said. "This scamp has just been telling me how much he missed all of us." She cocked her head toward Percy. "I didn't expect you to return alone. I thought—from your letters—that you had met someone ..."

"It didn't work out."

Georgina saw the wave of sadness pass over Percy's face, a look she recognized because that same sad look met her gaze in the mirror when her thoughts were consumed by Benjamin. Unrequited love.

She gave Percy's arm a quick, sympathetic squeeze. "I'm so sorry. Her loss, truly."

"Turns out it's a loss for both." As he spoke, Percy flashed her an understanding look. Clearly, the torch she'd carried for Benjamin these past years had not been as well-hidden as she had thought. She glanced at Henrietta, wondering if the other woman was also aware of her feelings for Benjamin.

"Now that you're back," Henrietta said, "we shall have to keep you so busy you have no time to miss her."

Georgina privately doubted it would be that easy. If the woman involved had shared Percy's feeling of affection, why hadn't things between them worked out? Then she reminded herself she wouldn't be around long enough to find out.

She turned to Percy. "I know you went first to Colorado Springs. Did you take the waters?"

"Indeed. The hot mineral pools are amazing. The Indians know where the best ones are, and will only take you there if you win their approval."

"How exciting!" Georgina said.

"Actually, the town itself can get depressing," Percy said. "Many of the hotels have been turned into sanatoriums for long-term guests. Folks who moved there for their health. And while their lives may be prolonged, they will never fully recover. The woman I ... I became enamored with—"

"Oh, no," Henrietta broke in. "Was she ill?"

"Not her," Percy said. "But she was caregiver to someone who was. She couldn't leave him. He had no one else, you see."

Georgina nodded. Unrequited love, just as she had suspected.

"At any rate," Percy said, "from there, I visited some colleagues on the east coast."

"Did it help?" Georgina asked, for his ears alone. "Getting away from—from everything else?"

"Not much, I'm afraid. Which is what brought me back here." His smile included Georgina as well as Henrietta. "Henny insisted I be here for the grand opening, and I felt compelled to ensure the opening was grander than anything anyone in these parts has seen before."

"You haven't changed a bit," Henrietta said gaily. "Once a showman, always a showman."

Georgina admired the brave face Percy put on for the sake of the others. She only hoped she could do so as well. "That's certainly your style."

"I also wanted to see with my own eyes that Hawkes is no longer wreaking havoc on the people who matter to me most."

"As far as we all know, Hawkes has met his maker," Georgina said.

Percy slanted her a look. "Men like that are never easy to kill."

❧

As Benjamin suspected she would, Georgina said her goodbyes to the bride and groom, then checked one last time in the kitchen before she tried to slip out the back entrance.

He caught up with her there. "You're not walking home by yourself. Not so long as there's breath in my body. Hawkes could still be out there some place, lying in wait."

"Marshal Philips doesn't believe that."

"Marshal Philips doesn't know everything," Benjamin said stubbornly, as he took her hand and tucked it in the crook of his elbow. Why had he never done this before? The move felt so natural. So right. He and Georgina walking arm in arm, his steps shortened to match hers as her shoulder brushed his arm. He took comfort from her nearness—at the same time his protective instincts were on full alert.

They continued in silence and had almost reached her

house before he spoke. "I can understand you wanting to sell the cafe. You've worked hard your whole life. It's time you sat back and took things easy for a change."

"I'm hardly one to sit back," Georgina said, with a laugh that somehow rang hollow. "This is my opportunity to make a major change. I heard about a logging camp up north that needs a cook."

"You won't like it there," Benjamin said flatly. "Rains all the time. Gray skies and everything damp and cold."

"I hope you're wrong," Georgina said. "Because they've offered me the job. And I plan to accept."

Benjamin's heart pounded. He was having difficulty breathing.

He couldn't imagine his life without Georgina.

When they reached her front steps, he turned toward her, pulled her into his arms and kissed her.

CHAPTER 3

Georgina stood passive in Benjamin's arms, resisting the urge to kiss him back. What was the point?

For years she had longed for him to look at her. To really see her as a woman. Imagined herself in his embrace.

And now, at the thought of losing her, he suddenly felt different? She knew better. Men didn't operate that way.

She'd witnessed the happenstance of love time and again as it hit each of the Mason brothers. Cupid's arrow had fully pierced each man's heart the first time they laid eyes on their intended, leaving them powerless to take their eyes from their beloved from that moment on. Even when Barron and Lily had been throwing daggers at each other, there had been a palpable heat between them, noticeable to anyone who bothered to take the time to see it.

And although his presence had always made her heart beat faster, Benjamin had never considered her more than wallpaper. A good listener. A confidante. A surrogate sister. Not someone to fall in love with.

Eventually he released her and stepped back half a pace to gaze at her. "Was it that bad?"

She let out a regretful sigh. "Goodbye, Ben." Then she turned and walked up the front steps of her house. The sooner the sale of the café was finalized and she was on her way to Seattle, the better. Because, lord help her, she wanted to stay. She wanted to run back into Benjamin's arms. To kiss him the way she had always dreamed of. To share the intimacies between a man and a woman she'd only read about in the forbidden book hidden in her home.

~

SHE WAS at home a few mornings later, penning her acceptance letter to the logging camp, when she heard a frantic pounding on her door. She peered out the side panel curtain to see Amanda pacing back and forth on the porch.

"Thank goodness!" Amanda burst into the room the second Georgina opened the door. "When you weren't at the café, I was afraid I might be too late."

"Too late for what?"

"To talk you out of leaving, of course," Amanda said.

"I'm not gone yet. Nor will I be changing my mind," Georgina said firmly. "The café is as good as sold. I'm accepting a job near Seattle."

"What about Ben? You'll break his heart," Amanda said reproachfully.

"I hardly think so."

"Look at Bradley and I," Amanda said. "I carried the torch for him forever. And then one day—"

"One day he was nearly killed by Hawkes," Georgina said dryly. "If that's what it takes to have Benjamin take notice of me, I want no part of it."

"Bradley noticed me long before that," Amanda said.

"He was just suffering some illogical idea that he wasn't worthy of me."

"Benjamin has never thought of me in those terms."

"Come on, Georgina. You know as well as I do what dense creatures men can be. Stick around. Give Ben a chance to show you he's serious in his affections."

Georgina gave Amanda a long, measured look. "Did you appreciate it when Brody stuck his nose into things between you and Bradley? Forced a betrothal on the two of you?"

"Of course not. But this is different."

"It isn't really. Now if you don't mind, I have to get to the café and check on things there. Then I have a letter to post."

"What about us?" Amanda wailed. "We're your sisters. We love you."

Georgina felt her resolve start to crumble. She lowered herself to the settee and patted the spot next to her. "Please don't make this any more difficult than it already is."

Amanda brightened as she took a seat. "If it's so difficult, how do you know it's the right thing? Shouldn't doing the right thing be easy?"

Georgina sighed. How to explain? "My entire life has been about doing the right thing for everyone else. My parents. The folks who work at the café. The customers. I put myself last because I thought that's all I was worth."

"Is that why you—"

"Go ahead and say it," Georgina said. "Didn't take pride in my appearance? Yes. Because I didn't think I was worth the bother."

Amanda cocked her head and scrutinized Georgina closely. "Something changed last year. *You* changed last year."

"Laura came to town. We spent time together as we planned the expansion at the café. She gave me something to aspire to. She gave me hope for the future. For the first time in my life, I felt good about who I was. Soon after that, I changed my hair and smartened my wardrobe. And at first it seemed to work. Benjamin noticed me and began to seek me out. He wanted to spend time with me." She shrugged. "More than a year later, you heard him. He considers me a sister. A friend."

"Tell me you're not leaving because of Benjamin."

"Not at all. I'm leaving because of me. Because I deserve more."

And because of Benjamin. Anything to avoid the heartache she would be forced to endure when she saw him with another woman. A woman who meant everything to him in ways Georgina never could.

Amanda leaned forward and gave her a long, heartfelt hug. "Thank you for explaining. It will make saying goodbye a little easier."

Georgina smiled. "Only a little?"

Amanda put her thumb and forefinger together so they were almost touching, only the tiniest crack of light between them. "As the Mexicans say, p*oquito*." She stood. "Now that I know your mind is truly made up, you must allow your sisters to throw you a going-away party."

"Oh, no. I couldn't."

Amanda placed her hands on her hips in a pose that brooked no argument. "I just heard you say you deserve more. In this instance, 'more' includes a going-away party with all your friends. Let others do for you for a change. After all, you're worth it."

With a final, no-point-arguing-with-me look, Amanda rose and let herself out, leaving Georgina to sit staring at the back of the door. Finally she rose, walked back to the desk and finished the letter to the logging camp. She stared at the missive for a long time before, with a determined sigh, she added her signature and slipped the letter into an envelope.

~

SHE WAS on her way to the post office later that day when she ran into Brody.

"Georgina," he said. "Just the lady I was looking for. When you weren't at the café, I was on my way over to your house."

Georgina grew wary. Brody was Laura's husband. Had he somehow got wind of the fact that Laura was her "angel investor" who had made the recent improvements at the café possible? "Oh?"

"Yeah. I had to come into town to pick up that crew of surveyors I hired to start mapping out the land back of Hawkes's. Figured I'd have a short word with you at the same time."

"What about?" Georgina asked as she fiddled with the handle of her bag. She'd known Brody ever since he moved to Bullet to live with his uncle Dan after his pa was killed, but despite being friends with his wife, she didn't feel she knew him well. He'd always struck her as a force to be reckoned with, the man who kept all the other Masons in line when it looked like they might be losing their perspective.

Benjamin always spoke of Brody with high regard, yet he gave the word "humble" new meaning with the way he seemed to feel everyone else on the ranch was a better man than he was.

"Doc Kennedy started the ball rolling the other night, and since then I've had more than a few people tell me I'd make a good mayor here in Bullet."

"I'd have to agree," Georgina said. "You're a natural

choice."

"I need to give it some thought, of course. But if I decide to take the plunge, I'll be needing an office here in town."

Georgina nodded, still wondering what any of this had to do with her.

"I thought you might be willing to rent me that little room out back of the café. The one where Rose stayed when she first came to town."

"Oh, I hardly think that would be—"

"I don't need much," Brody said.

"Wouldn't a room at the Institute be a better choice?"

"I thought about that. But there's too much going on there. I want someplace more private. A place folks can seek me out without feeling others are watching to see who comes and goes."

"Well I—"

"Just give it some thought, would you?"

"I would if I was planning to stay in Bullet," Georgina said. "But as it turns out, I have a party interested in buying both the café and the house." She waved the letter she was on her way to post. "And I have just accepted a job outside of Seattle."

Brody's jaw dropped. "You're leaving? Just like that?"

"I felt like it was time for a change." She was getting a little tired of having to defend her decision. First Amanda this morning, and now Brody. "I'll mention your interest in renting the back room to the purchaser. See if they have any plans for the space."

Brody shook his head. "I can't believe you're leaving. You're a fixture here. One of the originals."

She lifted her chin and met his gaze squarely. "Maybe I'm tired of being a fixture. Of being taken for granted."

His eyes narrowed, and he nodded to himself as if something puzzling suddenly made sense. "Ben's been moping around these last few days, acting like he just lost his best friend. I'm guessing you already broke the news to him."

"He's aware of my plans," Georgina said. "Amanda is as well, because she dropped by this morning to try and change my mind, so I'm quite certain word will be all over town before nightfall."

"I imagine it will," Brody said. "I'm sorry to see you go. You'll be missed."

"I think you becoming mayor here is only the first of a great many changes in Bullet. Soon no one will remember Georgina from the café."

"You're wrong about that." Brody extended a hand. "Let me be the first to wish you all the best."

She slid her hand into his. "Thank you, Brody. And to you in your new position as mayor."

"You sound pretty sure I'm going to take it."

"You're smart enough to know you can do a better job than anyone else here. And you care about the future of Bullet more than most."

Brody gave a rueful nod. "Sometimes it doesn't pay to care so much."

Georgina smiled in agreement. "I can't argue with you there."

She continued on to the post office in back of the stage coach office. The second she passed the postmaster her letter, she felt like snatching it back.

"Didn't know you knew folks up in Seattle," he said.

"We don't communicate often," Georgina said, hating that she felt forced into telling a lie. Which is exactly why starting over someplace new was a good idea. Someplace where no one knew her or her family and tried to make their business hers.

She kept repeating that to herself over the next few days without much success.

This feels more like it! Ben thought, as he saddled up and followed the others out of the barn. A project that included him and all his brothers. Brody had rounded them all up to head over to check on the survey crew. Ben wasn't sure how many surveyors were there, but the team had been here a few days. They were staying in tents out back of Hawkes's and mapping out the combined properties that had belonged to Hawkes and Ross with an eye to the best sites for housing.

Ben had overheard enough of Brody's pow-wows with the so-called "experts" to know the master plan involved keeping the living quarters a fair distance from the mine site, which would be on Copper Moon land. One factor still being bandied about was the best way to transport the workers to and from the mine over some pretty rough terrain.

The area behind Hawkes's was a hive of activity, with men coming and going, packing equipment that was totally foreign to Benjamin. Off in the distance, others were spaced out at intervals as far away as Ben could see.

"Marcus." Brody led their group to a large open tent and the man Ben assumed to be the head honcho. Brody looked around. "Looks like you expanded the crew since last time I was here."

Marcus nodded. "I hired a couple more. I know you want this done as soon as possible."

Brody nodded. "It's important we get it done fast but get it done right."

As Brody and the other man chatted, Ben's attention wandered. From what he could tell, most of the crew were going about their tasks in an efficient fashion. Curious to know what surveying was all about, he rode closer to a couple of the men, close enough to overhear them talking. The words "Red's gang" caught his ear, and he moseyed his mount closer, trying to pretend he wasn't listening.

Apparently he wasn't subtle enough. The fatter one elbowed the skinny one, who clamped his mouth shut immediately and started fiddling with a piece of equipment that reminded Ben of the twins' spyglass.

"Morning, fellas," he said in a casual tone.

The fat one grunted. The skinny one didn't say a word.

"Been over at the mine site yet?" he asked.

"Other crew's over there," tubs said.

"How long you think this'll take?" Ben asked.

"Ask the boss," he said. "We just do what we're told."

Ben nodded, tipped his hat and rode back to join the others. He'd been listening to his gut his whole life, and something about the pair didn't ring true. For sure, they bore watching.

When he brought the topic up to Brody later that day, Brody brushed him off. "Quit looking under rocks for something that's not there, Ben. Marcus's crew knows what they're doing."

"Marcus said he hired on some new guys. What if a couple of them are here under false pretenses? Believing those old stories about Red's Rowdies' last haul that has never surfaced?"

Brody blew out an impatient breath. "No one even knows if there's any truth to that old rumor that's been exaggerated over the years. We're moving forward into the future."

"Maybe that future doesn't hold a place for me."

Brody leveled him a long gaze. "That part's up to you."

Benjamin wheeled about and headed off in a different direction from the others. Behind him he heard a shout. Followed by Brody's voice. "Let him go."

Eventually he reached what he considered his "special place" on the far reaches of the ranch. Far as he knew, no one else had ever set foot here. It was the place where he sought refuge when something bothered him, something down deep. Like right now, feeling he had no purpose. He hated feeling this way. Not needed here. Not by anyone. Particularly not needed by Georgina, who was moving on with her life in a totally new direction.

He dismounted and pulled out his rifle. Everywhere he looked he saw evidence of his earlier visits, bullet holes in anything that could be considered a target. Shooting was the one thing he was good at. The one thing that brought him solace.

He didn't feel bad about the holes he'd shot in the saguaro cacti, for he knew that small birds would use them as birdhouses.

He was looking around, citing a new target, when a snake slithered out from behind a rock. Ben took aim. The creature was dead before it knew what hit it, and he kicked the lifeless body aside. He felt much the same, like all life had been snuffed out of him.

Usually he could force his mind elsewhere, same way he coped during his short stay in prison. But it wasn't working this time. His mind insisted on returning again and again to Georgina, widening that empty hole inside him that came from knowing she was leaving for good.

Lately, whenever he found himself riled up or out of sorts, Georgina had this special way of calming him down.

Her company was like a soothing balm on a festering wound. Just being around her filled him with peace. Made him feel like a better person than he was. He hadn't had need lately to reach for his rifle for solace. Not while he'd had Georgina.

He took a shot at a rock he'd painted a bull's-eye on. He'd never known who his real father was. Childhood had been a succession of different men coming and going, and he wasn't much more than knee-high to a grasshopper when one of those men had put a gun in his hand and taught him to shoot.

He'd taken to it like a duck took to water, and his ma seemed proud of his skill. He'd do anything to make his ma proud. He loved it when she called him her "little man."

He didn't stay little for long. He grew up fast, tall for his age, a gun never far from his hand, smart enough to know it was a bad move the night ma brought those two men home. He'd gone out rather than listen to her entertain them, and only got home in time to hear her crying and saying "no."

He'd walked in to see one of the bastards roll off of her and fasten his trousers while the second one climbed aboard. He'd killed that second man dead with his first shot. But ma's screams distracted him and the first man got away. The one he later learned was called Hawkes.

Even back then, Hawkes had the law in his pocket, for Ben was carted off to jail before he had time to take a piss. Eventually someone realized how young he was and that he'd been defending his ma.

By the time they let him out, ma was long gone. Ben filled his days making a living with his rifle and learning everything he could about Hawkes. Which is how he eventually ran into Brody and the others.

Having been a loner all his life, he'd been reluctant to

join their crusade. But Brody had a convincing way. And it was heartening to meet a group of men who all hated Hawkes as much as he did, each for reasons of his own.

Benjamin let off a volley of shots into the sky, startling a flock of birds who made a hasty retreat from his line of fire. He wished he'd stumble across Hawkes out here choking as the murdering, raping scum neared his last breath. Except that would bring up a difficult choice. To put the man out of his misery or sit by and enjoy watching him suffer.

At some point, with the desert his only witness, Ben felt a new resolve flow through him. Georgina was determined to leave, and it wasn't his place to talk her into staying or expect her to adjust her plans for him. But he could do the right thing, the gentlemanly thing, and make sure she got to her new destination safely. It was the least he could do.

He didn't stop at the ranch on his way in but kept riding toward Bullet. He didn't know how soon Georgina was fixing to leave, but it was important she knew she had his full support. And that he had her back. After all, that's what friends did!

She wasn't at the café when he stopped in. He guessed she'd already started to put some distance between herself and the business that had been her entire life to this point. Probably wise.

He rode around the corner from the café to the tidy house her parents had built, the house where Georgina had lived her entire life. He stared at the building's clapboard exterior, unable to imagine spending his entire life in one home. He'd lost track of how many different places he'd lived before he landed here, and couldn't fault Georgina for wanting to see a different part of this vast country.

He'd barely raised his hand and knocked when the door

opened and he found himself face-to-face with Brody's wife, Laura.

"Benjamin," she said. "What are you doing here?"

He felt like asking her the same thing. Except, over her shoulder, he saw the Mason brides Storm, Henrietta, Amanda, Lily and Rose were all gathered inside near Georgina.

"Appears I came at a bad time," he muttered.

Laura gave him a look filled with understanding. "Don't be silly. Would you like to come in?"

"I, uh—" Panic closed off his throat. The scene inside was unsettling. All his brothers' wives. And Georgina. One of them, but not really one of them. Not unless she was also married to a Mason. And he was the only one left.

"Never mind," Laura said kindly. "Wait here. I'll send Georgina out."

He opened his mouth to say he'd come back some other time, but he was too late. Laura was already gone. And as he stood there staring at the house, he realized he had no idea what he ought to say.

Even to him it sounded pretty arrogant to suggest Georgina wasn't capable of seeing herself safely across the country. She'd been looking after herself and everyone else around town for as long as he could remember.

Georgina knew him better than anyone. Well enough to see past his feeble excuse to spend a little more time with her. To pass his caring off under the guise of friendship. She deserved better. She deserved the truth.

And the truth was, if he could love anyone, Georgina would be that woman. But something must have happened further back than he could remember. Something that made it impossible for him to love anyone.

CHAPTER 4

L aura tapped Georgina on the shoulder. "Georgina, Ben's outside. He wants to talk to you."

Georgina wondered if her face had suddenly gone as pale as she felt.

"Did you tell him I'm busy?"

"I invited him in, but I could tell he didn't want to talk to you in front of all of us."

And Georgina didn't want to talk to him ever.

She was already choked up with emotion from her going-away party. Last thing she needed or wanted was Benjamin showing up at her door.

Reluctantly, she rose. Manners dictated she not leave him standing out there. These women were his sisters-in-law. They wouldn't understand why she longed to just pack up and leave without drawn-out teary goodbyes and best wishes for her future.

Especially without seeing Benjamin again.

Why had he kissed her the night of the wedding when she told him she was leaving?

There'd been nothing sisterly about that kiss. Nor was there any passion behind it. It felt like a duty kiss. She knew him well enough to sense his reluctance, his internal struggle, almost as if someone had put a gun to his head and forced him against his will to kiss her.

She slipped through the front door and closed it silently behind her. Benjamin stood staring at the street, his broad, capable back toward her, both hands clasped behind his back.

"I didn't mean to break into your hen party," he said, without turning around.

She knotted her hands together in front of her. How did he know she was there?

"You're welcome to come in. After all, you know everyone in there better than I do."

"I doubt that." He turned and removed his hat. "Got something that needs saying, for your ears alone." He cleared his throat.

Georgina felt an unexpected bubble of hope tickle her innards, before she dashed it away. Hope was a fool's game. "What's that?"

"Not sure when you plan to leave for Seattle, but I aim to come with you."

"You ... You what?" Her eyes searched his, but he gave away nothing of what he was thinking.

He nodded and plopped his hat back on his head. "It's the gentlemanly thing to do. Make sure you get there safe. None of the brothers would let their woman travel alone across the country."

"Ben," she said softly. "I'm not your woman. You're not responsible for me or for my safety."

"You've been a good friend," he said gruffly. "Seeing after each other is what friends do."

Did friends also engage in a passionless kiss?

Maybe other friends hugged freely and touched each other easily. What friends did not do was dream of the other friend, imagine his touch, conjure up his scent, his ...

She stared up at him in the dim light. How could he not know the way her heart raced whenever he was near? The way her breathing grew more difficult and tingly, while impossible-to-ignore prickles of awareness came to life in the most unexpected and embarrassing places on her body?

"So that's settled," he said.

Was that relief she saw cross his face?

Why not let him believe all this confusion could be so easily settled? After all, she'd spent years letting Ben believe what he wanted to.

"Good night," he added.

"Good night, Benjamin." Georgina sighed as he turned and walked toward his horse with that purposeful, long-legged stride she'd know anywhere. She watched him mount up and ride away with nary a backward glance.

This was her fault. She'd accepted Benjamin's friendship from the very start. She could hardly blame him because his feelings hadn't changed and grown the same way hers had.

She turned as the door behind her opened.

Storm joined her on the porch. "What did Ben want?"

"He insists on accompanying me to Seattle. To make sure I get there safely."

"He's always been a gentleman that way. He has this little boy side to him that he works hard to hide from the other men. But I see it when he thinks no one is looking. I'm not sure if it stems from his mother, because he never talks about her, but he sure is in need of someone to love and accept him just the way he is."

"I'm certain he'll meet that woman one day." Georgina forced an unconcerned smile. "All the other brothers did."

Storm linked her arm companionably through Georgina's. "Not an easy lot, those Mason men. They all have their secrets. Not to mention those gaping, invisible wounds that they try to pretend don't exist."

"Things should be better now with Hawkes out of the picture. After all, there will be exciting changes coming to Bullet."

Storm gave her a farseeing look. "It's a shame you won't be here to see those changes happen firsthand."

Georgina blinked back a wayward tear. "None of you has any excuse not to write and keep me apprised."

"Will you write back?" Storm asked.

Georgina nodded.

"And promise me one thing. If you're not happy there, you'll come back."

Georgina found herself nodding reluctantly. The last thing she envisioned was hightailing back to Bullet with her tail between her legs, directly into the path of her main reason for leaving in the first place.

"Guess why Ben was here, ladies," Storm said as she and Georgina returned inside.

"Don't tell me he finally came to his senses and realized Georgina is the one for him?" Henrietta said.

Georgina's heart fluttered so fast, she thought it might burst free. She forced a laugh. "Quite the contrary. He insists on escorting me safely to my destination."

"When are you leaving?" Lily asked.

"As soon as the new owners of the café return to sign the papers."

"Did you get part of the sale price up front?" Laura asked.

Georgina shook her head.

"Something in writing, at least?" Amanda said.

Georgina shook her head again.

The ladies fell silent. No one met her gaze. Georgina lowered herself into a nearby chair. "They seemed most sincere," she said. "A husband and wife from Mexico with two young children in tow."

"And they just approached you out of the blue?" Henrietta said. "Didn't you find that a bit odd?"

"Not at all," Georgina said. At the time she'd thought it was the answer to a prayer.

"And their offer was a generous one?" Laura said.

Georgina bit hard on her lower lip as she nodded. "Very generous."

Amanda perched on the arm of her chair and laid a comforting hand atop her shoulder. "I hate to say it, but I think perhaps you've been the victim of a con."

Georgina glanced from woman to woman. "A con? But how can that be? I gave them nothing."

Amanda patted her shoulder. "The twins have talked about this. It wasn't anything they ever pulled, but they saw it more than once in small western towns."

"She's right." Laura spoke up. "The con artists, usually a nice young couple, approach a business owner with an offer that seems too good to be true. The owner gets all excited, makes plans and commitments in preparation to sell and move on. That's when the couple returns with bad news. They're unable to raise the amount of their initial offer. They act all sorry and contrite, and bamboozle the business owner into accepting a ridiculously low offer."

"Who would fall for that?" Georgina said indignantly.

"Quite a few people, apparently. Folks who are ready to move on into a new life. Meanwhile, the con artists have a

KATHLEEN LAWLESS

new purchaser all lined up and waiting. They sell these new people the business for far more than they paid for it and off they go to find a new victim."

Georgina shook her head. "I find this all very hard to believe. Why would they approach me?"

"A woman on her own? That's their favorite victim, according to the twins. Generally speaking, women are new to business and, unfortunately, more gullible. With no husband or other family members to weigh in, a woman can be far more easily talked into taking the lesser price."

"I feel so foolish." Georgina glanced around the room at her friends. "Please promise me this conversation stays in this room. I couldn't bear for folks in town to know I'd been made a fool of."

One by one the ladies nodded in agreement, but she could tell they didn't like it. Easy for them. Each one had a husband looking out for their best interests. It was different being a woman on her own. Then she clipped off that thought. Every one of her friends had been on her own in one way or another before joining the Mason family.

"What will you tell the townsfolk?" Laura asked kindly.

"That I changed my mind," Georgina said simply. "Once I found out how cold and wet it is in Seattle."

The ladies glanced at each other and rose as one, as if given an invisible signal.

"Will you be all right?" Amanda asked, as they collected up their shawls and bonnets.

"Why wouldn't I be?" Georgina said. "You saved me from making a bigger fool of myself. This way I can save face and—"

And what? Settle more firmly into her life as a lonely spinster?

"And see firsthand all the wonderful changes ahead for our town," she said brightly. "Laura. Tell Brody he is welcome to use my back room for a mayor's office, anytime he's ready."

"He'll be happy to hear that," Laura said.

BENJAMIN DIDN'T BELIEVE in drowning his sorrows, but after leaving Georgina's house, he found himself in Bullet's only saloon, where he ordered a whiskey.

The bartender raised a brow. "Little early in the day for you, Ben, isn't it?"

Benjamin just sent him a dark look. "Can't a man order a drink when he feels like it?"

"Ignore the barkeep." Percy set down a glass as he claimed the stool next to him. "I know I do."

Ben's drink arrived and he took a swallow. Seemed it was impossible to be alone in a town the size of Bullet.

He turned to Percy. "I'm surprised you're still here. Figured you'd be off chasing a new hidden treasure on the other side of the world."

"Interesting assumption," Percy said, holding up his glass as if the answer lay within its contents. "Would you believe I missed you lot?"

"Isn't Bullet a little quiet for your tastes?"

"How about, I came back to help mend a broken heart, with the help of my friends?"

Ben did a double take. "I didn't think you..."

"Had a heart?" Percy said wryly.

Ben felt stupid. "Not that. I just didn't think ... You've never acted like there was room in your life for a woman, given the way you're always off gallivanting, or buried in your research papers."

"I'm as vulnerable as the next man when it comes to the charm and companionship of a special lady. Waxing poetic daydreams about seeing her life entwined with mine. Enjoying the many ways her presence makes my life complete. Elated when we're together and bereft when we're apart."

Ben tensed. In the part about her presence making his life complete, Percy was describing the way he felt about Georgina.

"What happened?" Ben asked finally. "Were your feelings not returned?"

"Quite the contrary, old chap. It's difficult to become firmly entrenched if such feelings are not mutual. That's when it becomes a fool's errand and necessary to move on. But when the lady in question feels the same way—" He sighed and took another sip of his drink.

A fool's errand, Ben thought. Did that describe his friendship with Georgina? If so, why was he having difficulty letting her go and moving on?

"Why are you here alone if this woman felt the same way you did?"

"Life's complications, my good man. She and I initially struck up a wonderful friendship, one I hoped would blossom into an eventual meshing of our lives."

Ben certainly hadn't felt that way about Georgina. Never thought of their friendship as being anything else. Until recently. Until she announced she was leaving. Suddenly, the thought of a future without her in it left him confused and unsure.

"And—" he prompted Percy.

"And it turned out the lady in question was unavailable."

"You didn't know that at the start?"

"Unfortunately, no."

"So you were misled." Ben felt a flash of anger for the duplicity of women. He'd been misled as well. Led to believe that his friendship with Georgina would always persevere.

"Not at all," Percy said. "I had seen her with said gentleman on innumerable occasions. It simply never occurred to me that they were husband and wife and she never offered up that information."

"But if she loves you, and not him—"

"She is nothing if not a loyal and caring person, one of her many admirable traits. She would never forsake her husband to be with another man."

"So the two of you are left miserable and apart."

"In a nutshell," Percy said. "I fear being around her, so near and yet so far, would only serve to increase my misery. Hence, here I am." He cocked a look toward Ben. "I imagine that's why Georgina's leaving town, don't you?"

"Oh, no. She— You're wrong about that. We've always just been friends. In fact, I plan to see her safely to Seattle. The gentlemanly thing to do and all."

Ben looked away when Percy gazed at him as if he was seeing far below the surface.

"Are you sure you're not prolonging your own misery in an effort to spend every last possible minute with her?" Percy asked.

"Nothing of the kind," Ben said shortly.

"Glad to hear it," Percy said. "For I wouldn't wish this abject misery on another soul. That reminds me. I ran into a fellow near Colorado. Not sure if it was you he was asking about or not. He didn't know your name, although the physical description fit. Along with the fact of you being the best sharpshooter in the west. Any ideas who it might be? And what he'd want with you?"

"Never been to Colorado," Ben said shortly.

Percy shrugged. "I didn't think so. Whoever he is, claimed the man he's looking for killed his father."

"I don't believe Georgina plans to sell the café and leave town after all," Storm told Blake as they packed up the book-lending wagon and started off for a few days on the road.

"That's good then?" Blake asked.

Storm smiled to herself. She loved her tall, strong, man-of-few-words husband and was grateful that he didn't try to dissuade her from taking books to folks who lived far away from the towns, choosing, instead, to accompany her. She had a short route she tried to get to from time to time, where they stopped at individual ranches where the wives were isolated and had no other company.

"Yes, darling, that's good. Now if only Benjamin would wake up and see what's directly under his nose."

Blake shrugged. "He'll come around in his own time."

"From what I saw at the wedding, he'll be having some competition from Marshal Philips. Which is maybe exactly what he needs to smarten up."

Blake wagged a teasing finger at her. "No interfering, my little Stormy one. And no matchmaking either."

Storm stuck out her tongue. "Spoil sport."

Eventually they pulled the wagon up to a homestead that Storm kindly thought of as dirt-poor, for it was much worse. Even the scrawny chickens scratching through the dust looked like they'd given up. She knew the wife had been a mail-order bride who had inherited a passel of young children. The woman's bully of a husband reminded Storm of that evil man she'd been married to before Blake.

Storm had barely hopped out to open the lending window on the side of the wagon when the door of the home opened. She turned to see not the wife, but the husband striding toward them with a menacing expression. Behind him, she saw a ripped curtain move at the shanty's only window, but no one else came outside.

"Get that wagon out of here. Yer not welcome!" the man said.

Instantly Storm felt Blake at her side, one hand protectively on her shoulder, the other holding his rifle.

"No harm intended, mister. My wife brought some books for your wife and young 'uns is all."

"Not no more," the man snarled. "Filling her head with rubbish and fancy dreams. The kids too. Staring at pictures instead of doing their chores. Ain't telling you again. Git! And stay away!"

As he spoke, he bore down on the two of them till he stood nose-to-nose, sneering at Blake. "Maybe if'n you were man enough to fill your wife's belly with your own brats you wouldn't be so worried about anyone else's. And she wouldn't have no time to be out here peddling her rubbish. If I see either of you around here again, I won't be so polite about it next time."

Blake cast Storm a worried look. She gnawed her lower lip as she cast one last look toward the shack, then gave her head a quick, jerky nod of agreement.

"Sorry for your trouble," Storm said, as she turned and

fastened the wooden shutter. Her heart was breaking, knowing what would happen to that wife once they left.

"Do you know the wife well?" Blake asked, once they were underway.

"Not very," Storm said. "Her name's Elsie, and her position is worse than mine ever was. Not only does she have a young one of her own, there are eight others she's forced to care for, every one of them as mean-spirited as their father. She worries what they might do to the baby."

Blake gave her knee a comforting squeeze. "I'm so glad you managed to get away, my love."

MORE THAN A WEEK went by without Ben hearing from Georgina as to when she planned to leave for Seattle. Surely it had to be soon. It was only fair he let Brody know he expected to be away for a time. Seemed things were getting more chaotic around the ranch as plans came together for the mining operation. Ben could barely get in or out of his bedroom in the ranch house without tripping over strangers coming and going.

Big family dinners were a thing of the past, seeing as the house had been turned into some sort of central meeting place where Brody was locked away much of the time with various mining experts, learning all he could about the pitfalls of extracting copper from the ground, and how to ensure the working environment was as safe as possible for the workers once the mine was operational.

There had also been a steady stream of builders and architects, all involved in plans for the land back of Hawkes's. Knowing Bullet couldn't handle a sudden influx of hundreds of miners, Brody was determined to do things right by supplying proper housing for the workers and their families.

Even though Ben had been the first one to complain about the lack of privacy in the house when he lived there with the others, he missed the way things used to be. Now that each brother had his own home with his wife, Ben found the ranch house lonely when it was full of strangers. And way too big for just one.

Inside the house, Ben found Brody alone for a change at the paper-strewn dining table.

"I know things are crazy right now, but I'm hoping you can manage without me for a spell," Ben said.

"What's up?" Brody pulled a stack of papers off the chair next to him so Ben could take a seat.

"I promised Georgina I'd escort her to Seattle and then out to that logging camp where she's fixing to work."

Brody got a funny look on his face. "Have you spoken to Georgina about this?'

"Not lately," Benjamin admitted. "I was waiting for her to let me know when she's getting set to leave." He straightened. "She hasn't left already has she?" The thought that Georgina might have slipped away without letting him know did unsettling things to his gut.

He slumped back down when Brody slowly shook his head.

"Georgina's still here. Matter of fact, it's my understanding she's not leaving after all."

"Not leaving?" Ben's heart gave a flutter. Dare he hope she was staying because of him? Had Percy been right after all? Then his hope plummeted. Percy had left because he couldn't claim the lady of his heart. Georgina leaving had nothing to do with Ben, no more than her decision to stay.

"Laura said Georgina figured the cold, wet weather in Seattle wouldn't suit her."

"I knew she'd hate that weather." Benjamin fell silent. The fact that Georgina had changed her mind about Seattle didn't necessarily mean she was fixing to stay here. There were lots of places she could light out to where it didn't rain all the time.

"Is she still selling the café?" Ben asked.

"Not to my knowledge. In fact, she said I could rent her back room. Turn it into a mayor's office when I'm ready."

"You planning to do this mayor thing, then?"

"I haven't fully decided. It's a ways off, if it happens at all. But I'm telling you one thing. If I become mayor, first thing I aim to do is to hire you as sheriff."

Ben stiffened. "I don't know the first thing about being a lawman."

"Doesn't matter. I need someone I know I can trust to keep things orderly around here. Someone who can't be bought. Someone who knows right from wrong and can outshoot anyone in his path should the need arise."

Ben stood. "I think you're giving me more credit than I deserve."

Brody gave him a rueful smile. "I know you, Ben. And I know there's no one I'd rather have at my side when it comes to a battle between good and bad. What else is going on?"

"Not quite sure where I fit in around here these days. Ranch appears busier than ever, yet nothing much seems to be happening. No one delivering or bringing back a herd the way we used to. Lots of comings and goings but nothing you need me for."

"Sorry, Ben," Brody said. "Things are a bit transitional

right now as we move in a different direction. I thought you'd be okay with a little extra time on your hands."

"Hmmph," Ben said. "Problem is, I don't feel like I'm pulling my weight." He knew Bradley kept busy with the animal stock and Blake was always tinkering on some gadget or another. Braydon had been consumed with helping Henrietta get the hotel up and running. And the twins—still on their honeymoon far as he could tell. Barely saw hide nor hair of either of them.

"I admit it feels strange not to be constantly looking over our shoulder wondering where Hawkes might strike next," Brody agreed. "Things will get back to a new normal pretty soon. If you have time, why don't you ride out and check on the fence lines and the herds?"

"Sure, Brody. Happy to." As he saddled up, a thought struck him.

Maybe it was time he moved on. He'd never stayed in one place as long as he had here. With Hawkes finally out of the way, he really had no reason to stay. Maybe he could convince Brody and the others to buy his share of the ranch. If not, maybe they'd let him stay on as a silent partner. Like Percy, it might be nice to feel he had someplace to come back to if he ever felt the urge.

Moving on would mean saying goodbye to Georgina. He hadn't relished the prospect when it was her doing the leaving. Would it be any easier if it was him packing up and leaving all this behind?

It ought to be easy. Moving on without a backward glance had never bothered him before. Why should this time be any different?

Because there were people here who he cared about. People he wanted to help protect. Even if they didn't need his protection.

He had barely started on his way when he saw Rose and

Lily come out of their respective cabins and head toward the barn. Was it his imagination, or were their movements furtive? Each gal lugged a bulging saddlebag.

He pulled back out of sight. When the two rode out of the stable in the direction of town, he decided the herd could wait till later. He wanted to see what the latest members of the family were up to that they didn't want anyone else to know about.

CHAPTER 5

Georgina's announcement to the café workers that she wouldn't be selling the business after all turned out to be a nonevent. She'd been expecting a barrage of questions, but all she got were agreeable nods before everyone went back to work. She found the same easy non-reaction around town, and once she told a few people, she stopped mentioning it. Life went on as usual.

Except for the notable absence of Benjamin. He used to pop in several times a week, usually after the customers and workers had left, when she was fixing to close up. When more than a week went by without any sign of him, she figured he'd heard the news and it had as little effect on him as everyone else.

The Mexican family had shown up a few days ago and the scenario played out exactly as predicted. So sorry they couldn't raise the full amount, but they still wanted to buy the business. Would she consider a lesser offer? Teary-eyed, they professed to having sold everything they owned in Mexico and borrowed from all their relatives to raise what little they were able.

Georgina hated to think what her response might have been had she not had the warning from her friends. She wished there was a way to stop the couple from preying on other unsuspecting business owners, but had to accept such unscrupulous dealings were out of her hands. She had firmly and unapologetically escorted them to the road out of town and suggested they not return to Bullet anytime soon.

No sooner had she seen the back end of the con artists, and life settled back down, than a suspicious-looking stranger showed up at the café. He sat at the back, shoveling in stew, his eyes darting about the place as if he was watching for someone. Georgina observed him for a while, wondering why his presence set off a warning signal. Had they all gotten too relaxed with Hawkes gone? What if Hawkes wasn't really dead? What if he'd sent this shady-looking young man to check things out and report back to him? It was just the type of move Hawkes would pull, one foot in the grave or not.

"See that man over there?" One of the waitresses pointed to the fellow Georgina had been watching. "He's asking a powerful lot of questions."

Georgina gave the young waitress a comforting pat on the shoulder. "Leave him to me. I don't want you ever serving anyone who makes you uncomfortable."

"Thanks, Miss G."

As the gal scampered off toward the kitchen, Georgina smiled to herself. She hadn't really noticed when it first started, but lately the folks who worked for her had taken to calling to her by her first initial, which she took as a sign of affection. She might not have family of her own, but these people were her surrogate family.

She picked up the coffee pot and walked over to the unkempt stranger. "More coffee, mister?"

Up close, she realized he was younger than she'd first guessed—his demeanor that of one much older, someone who'd had the life whipped out of him. He grunted and pushed his cup toward her.

Little light on the manners, Georgina thought as she topped up his coffee.

"I don't recall seeing you in these parts before. You staying a while or just passing through?"

"Depends." He let out a belch and pushed his empty stew plate to one side.

"Well, we have a nice new hotel down the street. Just opened the beginning of the year, if you're looking for a place to stay." She doubted he was the hotel-staying sort but thought a friendly overture might glean her some information.

He didn't say a word, just watched her from behind half-lowered lids. Scrape away that stubble on his chin, and she'd bet he hadn't seen twenty years. Little young to be a drifter, little old to be a runaway.

"You looking for work?" she asked. Because she'd happily tell him there was none and help hasten him on his way.

"Looking for a man," he said, finally.

"Are you a bounty hunter?" She hadn't imagined that same quiet, hungry look as when the occasional bounty hunter came through the door.

"Nope. Fellow I'm looking for just might be the best sharpshooter in all of Arizona."

Her thoughts flew immediately to Benjamin. "Most of the ranchers are no stranger to a rifle, but I've yet to see anyone with skills out of the ordinary. Does this man have a name?"

"Nope." He rose and dropped a few bills on the table. "Guess I'll be on my way then."

A FEW DAYS LATER, the café was having an extremely quiet day when Laura sought her out. With baby Charlotte on one hip, Laura appeared perturbed, which wasn't something Georgina was used to seeing. Normally Laura was serene and unflappable, a steadying influence on Brody and the others at the ranch.

"I don't suppose you have time to take a run into Yuma with me, do you? I have an appointment this afternoon and I'd rather not take Charlotte in with me."

"Leave her here," Georgina said. "I'll look after her."

Laura gave her head a quick shake. "She'll be due for a feeding right around the time I get there." She glanced over her shoulder. "I don't want Brody or the others to know where I'm going."

Georgina's curiosity was piqued. "Let me just tell the kitchen I'm stepping out for a few hours."

"Thank you, Georgina." Laura's relief was palpable, and Georgina felt honored to be in a position to help. "I didn't want to ask any of the other ladies because it's not fair to expect them to keep a secret from their husbands."

"No problems there for me," Georgina said. "Would you like me to drive?"

"Would you mind?" Laura said. "I'm a little distracted."

"Not at all."

In minutes they were underway. As she drove, Georgina slid the occasional sideways look at Laura when she thought the other woman wasn't looking, but she wasn't stealthy enough.

"I can't imagine what you must be thinking," Laura said finally. "And it's really not right to get you involved, either. You're practically family."

"Whatever you're about is none of my business," Georgina said. "I'm just happy to help."

"It's Brody," Laura blurted out. "I know he's stretched really thin since he bought out all Hawkes's debts and took over Hawkes's ranch, to say nothing of the scope of the mining project with housing for the workers and heaven knows what else is in the hopper. I want to help, but he won't even consider it."

"Oh, dear." Georgina stared straight ahead. "Is he aware ... Does he know... ?"

"What I'm involved with around town? No. When we got married, he told me I can do whatever I want with my money, but that he won't touch a dime of it. He's stubborn and proud, and I can't change his mind."

"Do you think he's afraid of what might happen if things don't work out with the mine?"

"Mining is always risky," Laura said. "But so is owning a hotel. Or a café. So is ranching for that matter. There are no guarantees."

Georgina nodded. "I understand. I remember how worried I was when you loaned me the money to expand the café. I don't think I slept for months until I felt certain your investment was secure."

"Brody is trying to do everything without outside investors, which is nearly impossible from what I can tell. I'd much rather he accepted the money from me than take his chances with the cards."

"Is that what you think he'll do?"

"He knows I never approved of him raising funds that way, but it seems to be the way he prefers to do things."

"I understand certain folks have strong feelings about the gaming tables," Georgina said.

"It's not that!" Laura spoke so loudly she woke her daughter, who let out a fretful cry. "Brody's father was killed when a game went bad. I'm worried the same thing could happen to Brody."

GEORGINA WAS ALONE in the café a few evenings later, still thinking about her trip to Yuma with Laura. She'd hated to discourage her friend after Laura had done so much for her, but she thought Laura's idea of enlisting a solicitor to help set up an investment company to approach Brody anonymously was a tad far-fetched, and the solicitor had agreed.

Men were so dashed stubborn. She was starting to see the decided advantages of remaining a spinster.

Georgina was getting ready to leave when she heard a knock at the door. Even before she opened it, she knew it was Benjamin. Not only did she recognize his knock, she could feel his presence on the other side of the door. Her heart sped up, her pulse raced and the hair lifted on the back of her neck. She peered into the mirror next to the door. Even her coloring was heightened. It was all she could do not to fling open the door and throw herself into his arms.

"Benjamin," she said, feigning surprise when she opened the door. "I was just about to lock up and go home."

"Got time for coffee with an old friend?" he asked.

She stifled a sigh as she drank in the sight of him, as dear and familiar as ever. Deceptively tall and lean, he was over six feet of sheer, solid muscle. His dark hair needed a trim and his eyes looked world-weary, as if he'd been kept awake with troubling thoughts. The day's growth of scruff on his chin accented his firm jaw and the slight hollow beneath his cheekbones.

Her heart shuddered, then sped up. Didn't he normally seek her out when something bothered him? What had brought him here tonight?

"Of course." He stepped inside and she closed the door behind him. His presence changed the café. No longer empty and lonely, the room felt cozy and welcoming as they moved to what she considered "their table." The place where they always sat. If her pulse had started clamoring before she opened the door, everything raced even faster as she faced him.

"I'll make some coffee," she said, anxious to have something to do with her hands. To stop herself from reaching for Benjamin. Making a right fool of herself.

She reminded herself he had been the one who kissed her that night, then disappeared from sight.

He reached out and caught her arm. The heat from his touch caused goosebumps in unlikely places. Like the crook of her elbow. The top of her shoulders.

Her gaze flew to his and her shoulder blades started to tingle. Rather than pull back, she shifted closer, her eyes never leaving his. His hands clasped her elbows, holding firm as he looked down at her. His warm breath ruffled the loose strands of hair framing her face. They stood so close a body could barely slide a sheet of paper between them. She felt the steady beat of his heart. Heard the ragged rise and fall of his breath before he spoke.

"Were you going to tell me you changed your mind about Seattle?"

Why should he care?

She ripped her gaze from his to stare intently at the

buttons fronting his shirt. "I figured you must already know, same as half the town."

"Brody told me. Why, Georgina?"

She forced a laugh and tried to step back, but his grip tightened. "Like you said, the weather wouldn't suit me, any more than cooking for scores of hungry loggers every day."

"You got someplace else in mind to move to?"

She gave her head a jerky shake. Bit her lower lip. "Why are you doing this? Holding me like this? Looking at me like this?"

"I'm fixing to kiss you. Would that be all right?"

Her heart skipped a beat. "You didn't ask last time."

"Last time I thought it might be my only chance."

Her mouth opened, but no words came out.

"I mean it, Georgina. I should have kissed you earlier and often. A fact I mean to make up for, starting now."

One finger under her chin raised her face to his, right before his lips glided over hers, gentle and coaxing, in a way she was powerless to refuse. When she began to tentatively kiss him back, he groaned heavy and low in the back of his throat and crushed her against him. His hands trembled as he gathered her close, as if he couldn't quite believe this was happening.

Neither could she. Her blood sang with the rightness of being in his arms. Her heart raced in approval as she tangled her hands through his thick, dark hair and fit her body against his—as if the two halves of a perfect whole had finally found each other.

It was a long time before the kiss ended. He held her softly, smiling down at her. "That was a whole lot better than last time."

"I never understood what prompted you to kiss me that night."

"Neither did I. At least not for sure."

"And this time?"

"This time I knew exactly."

"Oh, my." Her knees started to shake. She reached behind her for a chair and lowered herself into it.

Concern shadowed his handsome face. "Something wrong?"

"This is just... this is all rather sudden, don't you think?"

"Sudden! Heck, I was afraid I was too late."

Which didn't answer her question. "What exactly *are* your feelings toward me, Ben?"

He pushed a hand through his ruffled hair. His face took on a pained expression, as if talking about it was difficult. "You're a special lady. What we have between us, that's something special, too. I care about you. Why else would I insist on making sure you got to Seattle safe?"

"So you approve my decision not to leave? To carry on with things the way they were."

He nodded. "Things between us have always been good. And now that you're staying, nothing needs to change."

"I see."

His brow furrowed. "Did I say something wrong?"

"Being honest is never wrong."

At that exact second, the door to the café burst open. The young stranger who'd been here a few days ago advanced, his gun leveled at Benjamin.

"We're closed!" Georgina said, starting to rise. Benjamin pushed her back down and stepped between her and the stranger, his gun at the ready. She'd seen Benjamin in action often enough to know the newcomer, no matter how good he might be with a gun, was outmatched.

"Got business with you," the man told Benjamin, waving his gun.

"Never seen you before in my life," Benjamin drawled, as if unconcerned by the interruption.

"You're the one killed my pa."

"Who says?"

"You spent time in jail for it."

Georgina started. She didn't know Benjamin had been in jail. What other secrets was he keeping?

"I was defending a woman."

"A whore!" the younger man yelled.

A shot rang out. His gun flew across the room and the intruder dove to the ground. Benjamin advanced and stood over the downed man, his pistol raised.

"Make no mistake, if I wanted to hit you, you'd be bleeding all over the floor right now."

"What then?" the other man asked, his eyes wary.

"You don't be calling another man's mother a whore."

"I didn't know it was your ma," the young man said as he attempted to squirm backward. Step by step, Benjamin followed the man's pathetic attempts to wriggle away. When his attacker neared the open door, Benjamin's booted foot shot out and slammed the door shut, effectively trapping the other man.

Georgina watched the tableau unfold, saw the terror cross the younger man's face as he recognized the deadly intent in Benjamin's eyes.

"And had you known?"

"Please, mister. I shouldn't have come. I always thought—"

"Thought your old man was a good guy? That he was shot down in cold blood, instead of what actually happened? Him and his cohort forcing themselves on an unwilling woman."

"I'm sorry." The young man's voice rose shrilly in terror. "I made a mistake."

"Several," Benjamin said, his voice so cold, Georgina barely recognized it. "First, you believed the lies told to you by others. Second, you underestimated who you came gunning for. Those are the kinds of mistakes that get a man killed."

The young man whimpered as he wet himself. Georgina rose. She had seen and heard enough.

"This has gone far enough. Benjamin you've taught the young man a valuable lesson. Stand back and let him be on his way."

"I dunno," Benjamin said, as he took aim. "How can we be sure he isn't just like his old man? Someone who enjoys hurting women. Spewing his seed in them whether they want it or not."

"You can't be taking the law in your own hands. You're not one to shoot an unarmed man."

After a long, tension-filled moment, Benjamin booted the man at his feet. "Get out of here and don't come back. And clean up your mess."

The man scrambled to his hands and knees, whipped off his dirty jacket and mopped at the damp floor before he stumbled to his feet, wrenched open the door and disappeared into the night.

Georgina recoiled as Benjamin turned sad, vacant eyes her way. "You're wrong. I have no problem shooting an unarmed man. Never did."

Before she could respond he, too, disappeared out the door and into the darkness.

Georgina threw her hands to her head and dug her nails into her scalp in exasperation. Why was she even surprised?

It seemed every time Benjamin let down his guard, let her the tiniest bit close to him, he immediately bolted.

She moved to the kitchen and began to set things up for breakfast the next morning. She knew sleep would be a long time coming as she played and re-played in her mind everything Benjamin said and did tonight before they were interrupted.

First he'd taken hold of her as if he had every right to do so. The fact that she no longer planned to leave town must have triggered something in him. Then he'd announced his intention to kiss her.

When he finally did kiss her—oh, what a kiss! Her heart soared at the memory, the sheer joy of experiencing something that felt so right.

Maybe *she* had ruined things. Reacted badly. Saying it was sudden, when nothing could be further from the truth. It was only sudden to her because she never expected it to happen. Him wanting to kiss her.

Then she had to go and question him further. Try to qualify exactly what the kiss meant, what his intentions were, when she knew that wasn't Benjamin's way.

Never ask a man about his feelings!

She flopped down into a chair.

She had done this! *She* had pushed him away.

COULD he possibly make any more of a mess of things? Kissing Georgina had felt like the totally right thing to do. And judging from her response, she thought so as well. Then the talk started, which is when it all went sideways. Her asking about feelings. All that stuff he never knew the right response for. And, no matter what he might say, he knew deep down inside there was no right answer. He could talk himself around in circles all day and just keep making things worse than where they started off.

Then that intruder burst in. The fellow had no idea how lucky he was Georgina had been there. Benjamin would have just as soon dropped him in his tracks as look at him. What Georgina said about him not shooting an unarmed man—she had no idea. Which made it all the more obvious he wasn't worthy of a lady so fine.

Benjamin approached the ranch and rode down the driveway. As he rounded the last bend, he pulled up short. The ranch house was ablaze with lights, and an unfamiliar horse stood out front. Something was up.

Rather than ride directly into the stable, he dismounted a short distance away and approached the house on foot. The blinds stood open, giving him a clear view of all the menfolk gathered about the table, along with Marshal Philips.

Ben lowered his rifle with a sigh of relief. Even knowing Hawkes was dead, he couldn't quite shake the constant feeling of being on his guard.

"What's everyone doing still up?" he asked as he entered the house.

Brody gave him a look he couldn't quite read. "Glad you're here to hear this, Ben. Marshal has news."

Ben wasn't sure he could take any more surprises this evening, and right now he could feel the heaviness of the air around the table. "The office of mayor yours for the taking?" he asked, in an attempt to lighten the mood.

"This is something different," Brody said. Ben noticed no one made eye contact with him. Definitely more bad news.

The marshal cleared his throat. "I was just telling the others. Some of my men found Hawkes's body."

"Well, that's good news." Benjamin pulled out an empty chair, swung it around backward to the table and straddled it. "Where'd they come across his remains?"

"Short ways off the road. On a deserted stretch between Bullet and Yuma."

"I'm surprised he made it that far," Ben said. "Was he riddled with bullet holes?"

"He'd been clipped a few times, all right," Philips said. "But that's not what killed him. He'd been stabbed to death. Seven times."

"Seven times?" Benjamin said. "That a fact?"

"Seems quite the coincidence, as I sit here facing the seven of you. Knowing you all had a hate on for the man."

Benjamin blanched. "You think we did it?"

"That would be the obvious conclusion. Except for one small detail. From what we can tell, given the body's state of decomposition, he's been dead right around ten days, which jives with a report of him trying to steal someone's horse."

Ben felt the weight lift from his chest. "Which means he was killed at the same time Barron was saying "I do." Guess that lets any suspicion off us. We were all, every one of us, at the ceremony. You spoke with us."

"Exactly right," the marshal said. "You boys have about as airtight an alibi as you can get."

"Face it, marshal," Benjamin said. "Hawkes had more enemies than Arizona has cacti. Any one of them could have come across him and finished him off."

"I'm aware of that fact. It's just a funny thing about those seven stab wounds. Downright perplexing. Along with the fact that there's no trace of the murder weapon. The knife sheath Hawkes wore on his belt was empty, yet I have it on good authority he never took that knife off."

"Wouldn't that be fitting?" Benjamin said. "For Hawkes to have been killed by that very same knife?"

"I'm on your side here, fellas," Philips said. "So hear me out, what I'm about to say next."

"We're listening," Benjamin said. The others nodded.

"I'm thinking maybe you boys got yourselves another enemy. One who tried to make it look like you all killed Hawkes."

CHAPTER 6

After much soul-searching, Georgina decided it didn't matter whose fault it was that Benjamin took off the other night. She had had enough. More than enough. She was done with Benjamin blowing hot and cold by turns. First, he kissed her at the wedding with no warning or explanation, after which he acted like it never happened and went back to treating her like his sister. Even insisted on accompanying her to Seattle because that's what friends did for friends.

Then he stopped by the other night and shared that swoony kiss. Except he'd run off straight away after that misguided young man showed up, and she hadn't seen him since.

Marshal Philips had been by the café a few times in the past few days. She had a funny feeling maybe he was fixing to come calling and was assessing her level of interest before he declared himself. Men! Sometimes she figured the world would be a far simpler place without them in it.

She was just plumb tired. Tired of running the café. Tired of cranky customers. Tired of not doing something more meaningful with her life. Which was one of the reasons she'd been so keen when approached by the Mexican couple. Before they came around, she hadn't even thought about making a life someplace new.

She glanced up when the café door opened and smiled at the sight of a familiar face. Several, in fact, as Amanda, Storm, Laura and Henrietta all trooped in together.

"Are you here for lunch?" she asked, reaching for the menus.

"No. We've come to drag you away," Amanda said.

"Oh, but I can't..." She bit off her words. The café wasn't overly busy these days. Clearly the townsfolk were excited to have someplace new to go for their meals, and her patronage had been down ever since the hotel dining room opened.

She wasn't worried. She knew Brody was planning workers quarters out at Hawkes's ranch and that he intended to pay his miners a fair wage. Georgina fully expected she, along with everyone else in the town, would prosper from the new mining operation.

She smiled up at her friends. "Sounds like a great idea. I'd love to get away for an hour."

"Good. The carriage is right outside."

"Where are the babies?" she asked, as she collected her hat and followed the ladies outside.

Laura giggled. "We left them with Brody. He's just at the ranch house taking a few meetings."

Georgina blanched. "How did that go over?"

"He knows it's good for Charlotte to spend time with her pa."

Amanda spoke up. "Next time we plan to go out, it'll be Bradley's turn to play nurse maid."

Georgina gave her friends an admiring look. "You know,

I helped my folks at the café from the time I was old enough to toddle around, and I cherish those memories."

"Brody's already got his eye out for a horse for Charlotte. He can't wait to get her up in the saddle," Laura said.

Laura sounded so much more chipper than the last time Georgina had seen her, the day they went in to Yuma where Laura met with the solicitor.

"Where are Lily and Rose?" Georgina asked, as they all climbed into the carriage. "I haven't seen them around at all lately."

"Neither have we," said Laura.

"I think they have some secret mission," Henrietta said.

"They must," Amanda added. "Lots of whispering whenever I see them helping in the library."

"Did you hear they found Hawkes's body?" Storm asked, as Henrietta settled in next to her in the back.

"Yes. What a relief for everyone."

"I bet you didn't hear that he was stabbed seven times?" Amanda spoke up from the front seat, where she was sandwiched between Laura and Henrietta.

"I didn't know that. What did the marshal and his men make of it?" Amanda turned to face Georgina as she spoke. "He suggested to Brody that the Masons have a new enemy close by. Someone who tried to make it look like the brothers all killed him."

Georgina gasped. "Who would do such a thing?"

"We don't know," said Amanda, "but all of us are fed up looking over our shoulders every time we turn around."

"I don't blame you. Where are we off to?" Georgina asked as Laura started the carriage with a lurch, and they headed in the direction of the Copper Moon.

"We're going out to the old Hawkes ranch," Laura said. "We need to come up with something else to call it."

"Is anything happening out back yet?"

"Not yet," Amanda said. "Brody is waiting for the surveying to be finished. We're going to go take a look around the house itself."

"Whatever for? Surely none of you are thinking of moving there?"

"Oh, heavens no," Storm said. "The Copper Moon will always be home. But I was talking to the others about an idea I had. We thought we'd like to get you involved. If you're interested, that is."

Georgina was overwhelmed with admiration for her four friends. "Don't tell me you're considering a new project? It's not like a town hall, a hotel, a book-lending wagon and a library aren't enough to keep you occupied."

Laura laughed. "I know it sounds ridiculous. Storm, you tell her. It was your idea."

"Brody and the others are really focused on the ranches and the upcoming mining project. Meanwhile it occurred to me, to us really, that there is a perfectly good, quite roomy ranch house sitting there empty."

"I see," Georgina said, although she really didn't see. "Are you thinking about maybe turning it into a restaurant?"

"Heavens no," Storm said. "But I believe it would be a perfect haven for women who might otherwise have no place to go."

"You mean like a nursing home or sanatorium for women?" Georgina knew Amanda's mother had spent her last days in a sanatorium outside of Yuma, and while it had been hard having ma at home the last few months before she passed, Georgina wasn't sure she would have been able to put her mother into some sort of institution.

Storm blew out a breath. "When I ran off from my horrid husband, I had no place to go. I shudder to think what fate might have befallen me if I hadn't met Miss Millie and got to help her with the book wagon. That woman literally saved my life. Not only was I able to get away, I was able to start fresh."

Georgina nodded. She wasn't on the run, but the idea of a fresh start somewhere else had been appealing.

"There are a lot of mail-order brides in the West, as well as women who marry simply because they have no other choice," Storm said. "If it turns out, as it did in my case, that the man doesn't treat her well, the wife is well and truly stuck."

Georgina's eyes widened. "You're proposing to provide them someplace to live?"

Storm nodded. "Not forever, just temporarily. A safe place to stay where their husbands can't find them while the wives plan out what to do next."

"Don't husbands tend to have all the power?"

"Look at us," Laura said.

"Yes, but you're all married to wonderful men who love you and support what you're doing."

"That's true," Laura said. "But outside of that, the laws are changing— slowly, but changing none the less. Already women in Wyoming territory have the right to vote. I see a time in the future when all women will have that same right."

"You really think so?" Georgina asked.

Laura nodded emphatically. "Look around at things compared to our mothers' days. Not only are women now able to own property, open a bank account, or start a business, I predict lots more changes underway."

"If that's the case, why do you all feel this safe place for women is important?" Georgina asked.

Storm pressed her lips together. "A lot of men won't

cotton to the new ways. Some of them will take it out on the women. Those women will be just as trapped as they ever were. And even more in need of a safe place."

"Here we are!" Laura announced as she pulled the wagon to a halt in front of the ranch house. "Let's go take a look and see how feasible this crazy idea really is."

Georgina was the last to alight. She stood and stared at the front entrance. "You're right," she said. "It's time this ranch had a new name."

"And a new purpose," said the rest of them in unison.

BEN TOOK out his frustration on the rocks and cacti at his special shooting place. For the first time in his life he felt at loose ends. For nearly as long as he could remember, his sole purpose had been to get Hawkes. That purpose got a little blurred with other things once he threw his lot in here with the others, but in the end the result had been achieved. Hawkes had been sent to his maker. Not by Ben's own hand, but the man was no longer a scourge on any other innocent parties.

Which meant his work here was done and it was time to light out for someplace new. He could easily get work as a hired gun any place he chose. But if what Philips said was true, and a new enemy lurked in the shadows, he owed it to his adopted family to stay and watch their backs till this new threat was taken care of. Watching everyone's back is what he did. His only contribution to the family.

He thought back to the old days, before all the weddings and babies. Struck him how life had been simpler back then. The men didn't all get along all of the time, tempers flared and clashes occurred, but life, for the most part, ran pretty smooth.

He smiled, recalling the time he'd sat down to help Storm repair some of the books Hawkes and his men had all but destroyed. He'd felt good, being able to do something none of the others could. Not to feel superior, by any mind, but happy to help out. To make a difference. To brighten someone's day.

These days, as lone occupant of the ranch house, which had become pretty much Brody's office, he felt in the way every time he walked through to his bedroom, like he was interrupting.

And then there was Georgina.

What had he been thinking? That he was a regular man?

Georgina deserved more than him showing up and monopolizing her time whenever it suited him. She deserved a steady fellow, like the marshal. A man who was always on the right side of the law.

He aimed a shot toward the horizon in time to see a horse and rider appear, coming toward him in no type of hurry from what he could tell. Remembering what Philips had said about an unknown enemy, Benjamin lowered his rifle but kept a firm grip. As man and beast drew near, he recognized that friend of the marshal who'd shown up at the wedding. Doc Kennedy.

Once he got close, the other man stopped and dismounted. "What did that poor cactus ever do to you?" he asked in a friendly voice.

"How'd you find me?" Ben had never felt overly friendly toward Philips, which made Kennedy a total unknown, even if Brody had vouched for the man. Ben saw no reason to trust anyone from the government more than the next man.

"The others told me you'd likely be out here. Said it's where you go when the restless urge gets the better of you."

Ben blanched. So much for his private spot! "Who said that?"

"They all did." Kennedy cracked a rusty-looking smile. "Funny isn't it, the way folks often know us better than we know ourselves?"

"Not funny to me," Ben said. He gave the man a belligerent look. "You must be after something if you trailed me all the way out here."

Kennedy nodded. "Got Brody mostly talked around the idea of running for mayor here in Bullet. There will need to be an election, make it look democratic, but seems unlikely anyone will run against him."

Ben nodded, wondering what this had to do with him.

"He said he'll only take on the role if you agree to the job of sheriff."

"Trust me. No one wants me pinning on a badge."

"I beg to differ on that score."

"You don't know me. Neither do the others. Not really."
Not down deep in his soul.

"They trust you with their lives, and the lives of their loved ones. That's good enough for me."

Ben felt the tension leave his shoulders. Kennedy was right. The others did trust him. Georgina not only trusted him, she believed in him. So why didn't he believe in himself?

"Sorry to say I was born with an itchy trigger finger. I've killed men and enjoyed the act of it."

"Afraid you might kill again? For all the wrong reasons?"

"Shooting's the only thing I'm good at."

"A man who knows he can kill, but doesn't, is the best man for the job of sheriff." Kennedy walked up till he was nose to nose with Ben. "I look at you and I see myself twenty some years ago. I could out-shoot and out-deal anyone whose path crossed mine. I enjoyed the power that came with knowing those facts. These days I'm enjoying a different sort of power. Power vested in me by that fancy government office out in Tucson. I think, once you get used to being the sheriff in these parts, you'll enjoy the power that goes with the badge. It's different, mind. Before long you'll come to see that, in a lot of ways, it's better."

Benjamin cocked his head to study the man before him. Kennedy spoke to Ben as if they were equals. "What made you see things different?" he asked, finally.

"Met myself a sweet li'l gal. She had this soft, gentle way about her that tempered some of that darkness churning around my insides. She believed in me. Made me a better man.

"I won't say I don't miss the old ways. Got quite a thrill recently, enjoyed my part in helping clean Hawkes out at the gambling tables."

"Did you cheat?" Ben asked.

"Let's just say I made sure I won. Know what else?" Kennedy said.

"What's that?"

"I look in the mirror every morning when I shave. I happen to like the man looking back at me. There was a time, years back, when I couldn't make that claim."

Kennedy's gaze met Ben's, and Ben looked away. How did Kennedy know he didn't have much truck these days with the man staring back at him from the looking glass?

"That gal that runs the café," Kennedy said.

Ben stiffened. "What about her?"

"Special friend of yours, it would seem. Philips has been testing the waters with her, not getting very far."

"Why are you telling me this?" Ben said.

"No reason," Kennedy said. "It's nice to have a loyal friend. One who believes in you. You're luckier than most. You got a whole family believes in you. Counts on you."

And therein, Ben thought, lay the crux of the problem. He was dead afraid of letting everyone down.

BEN RODE into the barn and dismounted. He'd barely taken the saddle off his horse when he heard Bradley call out from a stall in the back. "That you, Ben? Can I get a hand over here?"

"Sure thing! Where are you?"

"Last stall, center. Wash your hands first."

Ben ducked out to the well, washed up and headed back inside, where he heard an unearthly sound of an animal in distress. He recalled Bradley had been keeping an eye on one of the mares who was due to foal soon.

"How's she doing?" The stall was well-lit from a nearby lantern, the birthing kit close by.

"Not too well. Her water hasn't broken, but the foal is coming." Bradley was squatted at the side of the mare, whose distended belly rippled with movement. Despite his soothing tones as he spoke to the horse, her eyes rolled back in her head and her breathing was agitated.

"Uh-oh," Bradley said. "Red bag! Hand me those scissors."

Sure enough, instead of a white showing of placenta near the mare's opening, Benjamin saw the deadly red sac, which meant oxygen to the foal was being cut off. He grabbed the scissors, passed them over, and knelt next to Bradley. "What can I do?"

Skillfully Bradley cut open the placenta and reached inside to help guide the foal out. "The foal won't be getting any oxygen. I'll give it a hand out. I need you to keep the mare calm."

"Keep her calm how?"

"Pretend she's a woman," Bradley said.

Ben swallowed thickly as Bradley's arms disappeared up to the elbow inside the mare.

"Talk nice to her," Bradley said. "Amanda had a tough time because Samuel was lying sideways, but I talked her through it and doc got him turned at the last minute."

The mare snorted and tried to get up.

Ben thought of Georgina as he dropped his voice to a soothing tone and started murmuring incomprehensible syllables and half-words, while he stroked the mare's head. She immediately calmed and once the foal started to appear, the mare began to nicker.

"That's good," Bradley said, his voice strained. "She's got all the right instincts for her baby. A mother's encouragement goes a long way at a time like this. Bonding can make all the difference. Luckily it's not her first time being a mom."

One more move on the part of Bradley, and the foal was fully expelled.

"Will it be okay?" Ben asked.

Bradley sat back and wiped the sweat from his forehead with the back of his forearm. "Time will tell. We'll see how long before he tries to stand."

As he spoke, the foal stumbled and wobbled his way to his feet.

"Good. The umbilical cord separated on its own," Bradley said. "Can you pass me that cup of iodine?"

As Bradley dipped the umbilical stump, the foal started to make sucking motions with his tiny mouth.

"Shouldn't he start nursing right away?"

"Not necessarily. I'll keep an eye and make sure he tries in the next hour or so. But his suck reflex looks good."

Bradley handed the iodine back to Ben, who set it out of the way of being knocked over. The foal took a few unsteady steps to its mother. The mare nuzzled her baby and eyed Benjamin, as if to ask what he was doing here at such a private moment.

"Her protective instincts are strong," Bradley said. "Probably best if you take off."

"What? Oh, sure." Benjamin stood. "What was it like when Amanda had Samuel?"

Bradley's entire face lit up. "It was a thousand times more special than what you just saw here. Makes me love my wife more every single day."

Benjamin swallowed the lump in his throat as he turned away. Bradley belonged here. He didn't.

"Ben?"

He turned back.

"Thanks for your help tonight. You did good."

"Glad I could help."

Benjamin saw to his horse and left the barn feeling good about his part in helping Bradley deliver the new foal. With all those fuzzy warm feelings running through him, he realized the one person he longed to share them with was Georgina.

Maybe he'd get cleaned up and head into town after supper. If she wasn't busy at the café, they could do something together. But what? He hadn't been paying attention to what went on at the Women's Institute. Maybe there was a lecture or a show or something Georgina would enjoy. He'd check with Amanda and find out.

As he approached the cabin Amanda shared with Bradley and their son, one of six new homes that had been built for each newlywed couple over the last year and a half, he wondered what it felt like to have a place that was well and truly your own. Along with your wife there waiting at the end of a long day.

He tried to picture himself in that scenario, making his way to his own place. He could see it clear in his mind, Georgina opening the door and throwing her arms around him, glad he was home. The idea brought a smile to his face. Maybe he wasn't such a confirmed bachelor after all.

He knocked on the door, expecting to see Amanda. When the door opened to reveal Georgina on the other side, he all but fell off his boots. He blinked once or twice, barely able to believe his eyes. Then decided, if this was a dream, why bother waking up?

He stepped inside and took Georgina into his arms.

CHAPTER 7

At first, Georgina stiffened when Benjamin stepped inside and took her in his arms, but slowly she relaxed against him. Being held close like this felt as natural as breathing. His heart beat solidly against her bosom while his warm breath stirred the hair on the top of her head. His fingers splayed against the back of her skull, holding her close.

She felt a shuddery sigh ripple through his body, the deep, contented sigh of a man who has finally come home. Could she settle for this? A Benjamin who needed her, even though he didn't love her? Maybe she was foolish to expect passion at her age. Maybe companionship was as much as she could expect.

"What are you doing here?" he asked, not letting her escape, one arm curled possessively around her waist.

"Watching Samuel for a bit."

"Where's Amanda?"

"She went down to the barn to check on Bradley. He has a mare due to foal."

"Everything worked out fine," Benjamin said. "It was

touch and go for a while there, but mother and baby are doing well. I left Bradley watching over the newborn as he tried to find his legs and his ma's teat, in that order."

She craned her neck to meet his gaze. "You were there helping?"

He shrugged. "I don't know how much help I was, but I was there."

Just then, Georgina heard a squawking noise from the back bedroom. "His highness is awake. Let's hope he's wet and not hungry. I'm a poor substitute for his ma if he's looking to feed."

Benjamin stroked her cheek with an unsteady hand. There was a look in his eye she hadn't seen before. A vulnerability, along with something else. A sense of purpose, perhaps?

"You're not a substitute, let alone a poor one. You're everything..."

Gently Georgina freed herself from his embrace and went to get the baby, who was indeed soaked through. She changed his diaper and pulled out a fresh crib sheet automatically, her mind still focused on Ben's words. What did he mean by "you're everything"? And did she only imagine his softly whispered words ... "a man could want"?

Little Samuel gave her an engaging, toothless grin, a clear sign that he wasn't in the least bit sleepy but had decided it was time to get up and play.

"So that's the way of things, is it, young man?" she said as she returned to the kitchen, the babe tucked against her.

Ben stood where she'd left him, a bemused look on his face as he watched her with the baby. "You're a natural." When his expression darkened, Georgina knew he was thinking of his own mother. "Not all women are."

"He's a very easy baby," Georgina said as she tickled little Samuel under his chin and made him giggle.

Ben's face was unreadable. "Little tyke doesn't know how lucky he is to have a ma and pa who dote on him."

"One day he will."

"Georgina, I—" Whatever he'd been about to say was lost when the door opened to admit Bradley and Amanda.

"Ben," Amanda said with a bright smile as she held out her hands to relieve Georgina of the baby. "Bradley said you were a wonderful help with the foal. Thank you for being there."

"It was nothing," Benjamin said. "Happy I could help."

"Well, you can be my assistant any time," Bradley said.

Benjamin cleared his throat. "Might not be around the ranch as much pretty soon."

Georgina's heart lurched. Her eyes flew toward him. Was he leaving?

"Nothing's for sure yet, but if Brody decides to put on his mayor hat, he's asked me to pin a star on my chest and fill the sheriff's job."

Georgina felt a rush of relief. "That's wonderful. You're a natural choice."

Ben turned to Georgina. "Would it be all right if I saw you home? When you're of a mind to leave, I mean. There's no rush."

"Actually, it's past time I returned to town," Georgina said. "I would love if you could see me back. I came out with Laura and some of the others."

"Lady business," Bradley said with a twinkle in his eye. "The wives are cooking up another project, but they won't tell us what."

Amanda gave him a playful swat on his arm. "We'll fill you in when the time is right."

"Be careful out there," Bradley told Benjamin as they left. "Remember what Philips said."

"What did Marshal Philips say?" Georgina asked, once Benjamin had her settled in the carriage and they were on their way.

Benjamin took his time answering, but she noticed his rifle lay across his lap, not far from hand as he drove. "Hawkes is dead, but Philips thinks we could have a new enemy. Which is always worse when you don't know who it is."

"Why does the marshal think that?"

Ben's answer was a little vague for her liking. "Just something to do with the way Hawkes died. Could mean nothing."

"Marshal Philips doesn't strike me as a man given to flights of fancy," Georgina said primly.

Benjamin cleared his throat as if uncomfortable. "It's not my place, but I gotta ask. How *does* Philips strike you?"

She gave him a sideways look. "I—I'm not sure what you mean."

"You two sat together at the wedding. I hear he's no stranger at the café these days, either."

"Benjamin Mason, I would think you have better things to occupy your time than listen to town gossip."

He pulled the rig to a stop and turned to face her. "You didn't answer my question. Does the marshal have any chance if he has wooing on his mind?"

Georgina twisted her hands in her lap. She'd never been one to take a chance, to throw caution to the winds. She drew a deep breath and faced her fears. Her life was at a crossroad, and everything that happened from here on depended on what she said and did next.

Resolutely, she turned to face Benjamin. "There's only

one man I'm interested in being wooed by. I know you don't love me. And that ours wouldn't be a passionate union, but we get along well, and I think—" The rest of her words were lost as Benjamin let out a growl and pulled her to him.

"You want passion? I'll show you passion!"

His kiss this time was everything she'd dreamed of and nothing she ever could have imagined. By turns tender and seeking, shy and then bold, possessive and hungry. The passion with which his mouth plundered hers took away her breath and whisked her to unscaled heights until, emboldened, she strove to meet and match his needs, his wants and his desires with her own.

Loneliness and diminished self-worth evaporated. And as Benjamin laid his soul bare to her with that kiss, she sensed everything he was revealing. His own loneliness. His need. His fear. His desire.

Oh, the passion! She was light-headed by the time he finally reined in the fervor, gentled the kiss, and eventually released her, keeping her close.

Her heart thudded against his as she dragged air into her lungs. Her head found its way to his shoulder. He pressed a myriad of kisses to the top of her head before he tilted her face up to catch sight of her in the moonlight.

"Passionate enough for you?"

She raised an unsteady hand to her throbbing lips. "I believe so."

"Good." He started up the carriage, and they made the rest of the trip to Bullet in comfortable silence. When they arrived at her house, he sprang from the carriage, loped around to her side and lifted her down as if she was the most precious thing in the world. She thrilled to the possessive feel of his arm around her shoulders as he walked her to the door, where he kissed her again, more restrained this time.

"I'll see you tomorrow," he said.

"What's tomorrow?"

He gave her a bemused smile. "You'll see."

WHY DID he have to go and bring up tomorrow? Now he had to come up with something special. Something to show Georgina that he was sincere. A fine lady like her deserved gentle and romantic wooing. Trouble was, he had no idea what that might entail.

As he passed the saloon, he spotted Marshal Philips's horse out front and impulsively drew to a stop. He hitched the horse and carriage to the rail, and went in search of the lawman.

"I'm surprised you're still in town," he said as he joined Philips at the bar and ordered a drink he didn't really want. "Heard Kennedy lit out back to Tucson. Figured you were with him."

Philips took a swallow of his whiskey. "In actual fact, I plan to stick around a while."

Benjamin cocked his head. "You got a lead on whoever might have it out for us?"

"Nothing yet."

Benjamin snorted. "What kind of lawman are you, anyway?"

"The kind who gathers the facts instead of racing off half-cocked, making a mess of things."

"Who's making a mess of things?" Benjamin blustered.

"Other than you with Miss Georgina? No one, far as I can see."

"For your information, that's all been taken care of."

"Is that so?" Philips signaled for another whiskey. "I guess we'll find out."

"Find out what?" Benjamin said.

"Whose style the lady prefers."

Benjamin narrowed his gaze. "Now see here. I've already staked my claim. Her and I, we have an understanding."

"The way I hear it, Georgina is still a free agent, free to make up her own mind."

Benjamin's hands curled into fists. "You heard wrong."

Philips shot him a cocky look and clinked his glass against Benjamin's. "May the best man win!"

Benjamin had no taste for the whiskey in his glass. He knew a challenge when he heard one, and for once in his life his skill with a rifle wasn't worth a hill of beans. He'd never felt so inadequate. He had no idea how to fight for Georgina.

HE RETURNED to Bullet bright and early the next morning, a bouquet of flowers in one hand, as suggested by Braydon and seconded by Henrietta. He knocked loudly a second time but the house remained silent. After a third, futile try he took himself around to the café, where he found Georgina bustling busily about the premises.

"I told you I'd be by today," he said.

"Yes, but you didn't ask about my plans," she said. "Turns out I'm needed here. Maisie's little one is sick so she stayed home with her and we're short-handed."

Ben stared at the flowers in his hand. "These are for you!" Awkwardly, he thrust the bouquet toward her.

She glanced around for a spot to put down the dirty

dishes she was carrying into the kitchen. "Thank you," she said. "I'll just put them over here with these others."

That's when he noticed the mason jar at the end of the dining bar, bursting with an array of colorful blooms that made his own offering pale in comparison.

He didn't need to ask who they were from. He knew! Philips had beat him here. He cleared his throat.

"How about, once you're done here, we take a spin into Yuma? Grab a bite at the hotel there?"

"I'd love to," she said. "Unfortunately, I have plans later. Marshal Philips is taking me to see that play over at the Women's Institute. It's supposed to be really funny."

"Hmmph," Benjamin said.

"Don't be like that." She flicked a playful finger at a button in the center of his chest.

"I thought we—I thought we had an agreement. I mean, last night—"

"Last night was magical," she said. "Things just happen to look different in the cold light of day. You blow hot and cold around me all the time. How do I know this time will be any different?"

"I thought I made that clear."

Georgina let out a sigh. "Unfortunately, Benjamin, with you, nothing is ever clear. Thank you for the flowers. Now if you'll excuse me, I have to get back to work."

Benjamin watched her weave through the tables, greeting customers and topping up coffee cups. His gut clenched as he heard her let out a hearty laugh at something one of the men said to her. Danged if he'd ever figure out women!

Deflated, he headed for the hotel, where he found Henrietta and Braydon in the ballroom. The room looked totally different from the night of Barron and Lily's wedding.

Henrietta held a paper in one hand and pointed with the other, as if they were mapping out the area.

She looked up when he entered the room. "Morning, Ben. How did Georgina like the flowers?"

"Okay, I guess," Ben said. "Turns out she's got plans with the marshal later on."

He didn't miss the way Henrietta and Braydon exchanged a glance. "What?" he said defensively.

"I was just going to say," Henrietta said. "If the marshal's throwing his hat in the ring to win Georgina over, you'll need to up your game."

"I don't understand it," Ben said. "Last night it seemed like things between us were finally going to work out. That we'd do stuff together. Hang out and—"

"Did you make solid plans?" Braydon asked.

"Not exactly," Ben mumbled. "Not yet, anyway."

"You mean," Henrietta said, "you just took it for granted that Georgina would sit around waiting for you to show up on your time and your terms, same as in the past?"

Ben scuffed the toe of one boot on the polished floorboard beneath his feet. "I guess."

Braydon clapped him on the back. "One thing I learned from this one here, my friend. Never take a lady for granted."

Henrietta threw Braydon a playful look. "It was a hard lesson to get through that thick skull of yours."

Through the banter, Benjamin heard the love and caring in their words to each other. He wanted the same, easy back-and-forth with Georgina. He just had no clue how to get it.

~

Braydon watched Benjamin's dejected air as he left the hotel and swung himself into the saddle. "You sure we're doing the right thing, my love? I know you had a little chat with Georgina earlier."

"Darn right!" Henrietta said. "You said it yourself. Ben has always taken everything about Georgina for granted. Just because he says he's going to change doesn't necessarily make it so."

"You don't think this is taking things a little far? Her encouraging the marshal?"

She poked a playful finger in his chest. "Who was the man who bragged to all his brothers how he'd have me eating out of his hand? If that wasn't taking things for granted ..."

"You taught me a lesson there my love. Turned the tables quite effectively."

"Georgina has to do the same thing with Ben. She can't simply fall into his arms now, just because he's ready. Actions speak louder than words."

"You women really know how to make us menfolk suffer, don't you?"

Henrietta leaned forward and kissed his cheek. "Which makes it all the more fun to kiss it better afterward."

Benjamin took an aimless ride through the streets of Bullet. The town had never looked better, all spruced and shiny, almost as if it was holding its breath in anticipation of more good things on the horizon. The hotel had been a major undertaking, but the locals had embraced it and travelers were starting to find their way here, curious about the town that started its life as a place where outlaws killed their victims with no intervention from the law.

Benjamin rode past a tour wagon from Yuma. The driver spoke into a megaphone and pointed out some of the sights, like the park and the town square, along with the Women's Institute that Amanda had spearheaded. He had to hand it to his sisters-in-law. They had had quite the impact around the place, and something told him they were far from finished yet.

Farther down the street, the driver pulled the tour wagon to a stop in front of the café where his passengers disembarked. Benjamin expected there would be a run on the popular new ice cream Georgina had started serving, along with her fancy new-fangled doughnuts. As he looked around, he expelled a breath of pride. This was his town. His home.

Just then, he spotted Lily and Rose riding into town. Like last time when he followed them, they rode through the park, around the gazebo in its center, toward the river. He'd hung back last time, wishing he had the spyglass with him. Far as he could tell they weren't doing much, just kind of got off their horses and started mucking around back there. Today looked no different. He gave his head a shake. Clearly, he'd never understand women.

CHAPTER 8

The play at the institute hall was as entertaining as promised. Marshal Philips once again proved himself an attentive, interesting companion, but Georgina was unable to concentrate. Her mind kept drifting toward Benjamin and how unhappy he'd looked when he left the café earlier.

Rather than concentrate on the play unfolding on stage, she recalled her chat with Henrietta earlier in the day.

"Was I too hard on Benjamin?"

"Not in the least," Henrietta had said, reminding Georgina how tough she had been with Braydon when she learned he'd made a wager with his brothers as far as winning her over.

"If anything," Henrietta added, "you've been far too accommodating. It's well past time it becomes all about you." She changed the subject. "Are you sorry the sale of the café fell through?"

"In some ways," Georgina said. She waved an expansive hand to encompass the hotel as a whole. "This was your dream and you made it a reality."

"Ohhhhh," Henrietta said, knowingly. "And the café was never your dream."

Georgina shrugged. "I couldn't bear to disappoint the town by shutting it down after pa died. People have been good to me and my folks over the years. And the town needed a café."

"So instead, you expanded," Henrietta said. "Helped grow the legacy you felt duty-bound to carry on."

Georgina had sighed enviously as she took in Henrietta's dream come to life. "You've known so much freedom. You've seen places most folks only dream about. Done whatever took your fancy."

Henrietta cocked her head to one side. "What would you do if you had the choice?"

"I don't know," Georgina said. "All I know is it would be nice to have the choice."

"You could close the café, you know," Henrietta said.

"Oh, I couldn't do that," Georgina said quickly. "The customers. The people who work there. They depend on me."

Henrietta nodded. "Same as Benjamin. It's high time folks stopped depending on good old Georgina to never let them down. It's past time they learned to depend on themselves."

Georgina blinked back to the present as folks around them in the hall started to applaud. Automatically, she clapped her hands together as she smiled over at Marshal Philips. He was a nice man. It wasn't his fault he wasn't Benjamin.

"Did you enjoy that?" he asked, as he helped her with her shawl.

"Very much," she said. Theirs had been the perfect date because it didn't require her to make conversation.

"It's a fine evening," he said as they stepped outside and he tucked her arm through his.

Georgina stared up at the sky. Was it her imagination, or did the stars always shine a little more brightly when she was with Benjamin? In spite of herself, she sighed.

Marshal Philips patted her hand in a reassuring way and remained blessedly silent as he saw her to her front door.

When they reached the porch, Georgina turned to him and asked, "Do you have a lot of people who depend on you?"

Philips pressed his lips together. "Depends what you mean. I have no close kin. I guess, in many ways, folks in the territory depend on me to see justice carried out."

Georgina nodded. Put like that, it sounded important. "I had a nice time this evening. Thank you for asking me."

"I can promise you, it won't be the last time." He leaned in to kiss her, giving her lots of time to step back if she chose. She didn't step back, but she did turn her face so his lips grazed her cheek instead of landing on her mouth.

He rested both hands on her shoulders and studied her face in the moonlight. "I take that to mean you only want to be friends."

Georgina let out the breath she had been holding. "Thank you for understanding." She knotted her hands together in front of her. "I wish it was different."

"One thing I learned is that we can't always choose the direction our heart takes us."

Georgina nodded. One more choice taken away from her.

"The other night I told Benjamin, "May the best man win." He winked at Georgina. "Don't make it too easy for him. Make him work for it."

She smiled. "You're the second person today to say as much."

"That's because you've got a soft-hearted nature. Good night, Georgina."

"Good night, Charles."

～

BRODY WAS ALREADY SEATED at the table when Benjamin came down the stairs the next morning. "What are your plans for the day?"

Benjamin blew out a breath. Not an ounce of privacy for a man in his own home, ever since Brody had taken over the main floor of the ranch house as some sort of operations center for the proposed mine and housing development needed to accommodate the anticipated influx of workers to the area.

"Going out and check the herds," he said brusquely as he started for the door, then stopped. "What's that you got there?"

The paper in front of Brody was old and yellowed, a far cry from most of the shiny new plans and diagrams Ben was used to seeing him hunched over.

"You remember all the hub bub last year about a map that Amanda's ma got from her pa? How Hawkes went a little crazy trying to get his hands on it?"

"And blew up her house when he couldn't find it?" Ben said.

"With Hawkes dead, Amanda asked me to figure where this is on the ranch and see if there's any buried treasure from the old outlaw days of her pa riding with Red's Rowdies."

"Didn't Laura try that? Almost got killed by Hawkes for her trouble."

Brody nodded. "The river's changed course over the years. I think Hawkes got spooked because Laura was close to stumbling on the shallow grave of the gang members he had killed."

"I thought you said it was all just rumors."

"I haven't convinced Amanda of that. She'd love to see the spoils, if there are any, returned to their rightful owners."

Ben moved to stand behind Brody and study the map. "You really think the gang might have hid the cache from their last heist before Hawkes killed them?"

Brody shrugged. "Could be Hawkes killed the others when they wouldn't tell him where the spoils were hidden. It also stands to reason, since he was planning to pretend to go straight, he wouldn't want anyone around who could implicate him later on or connect him to the stolen loot."

"Wasn't there talk at one point of passing this map over to Percy to see if he could figure it out? Him being an experienced treasure hunter and all."

"Amanda and I agreed it's better to keep this in the family. She doesn't want some stranger stumbling over it once we start working the copper mine."

"You want to go exploring? See what we can find?" Ben asked.

Brody got to his feet. "I was hoping you'd say that."

Ben knew Brody counted on him when it looked like he could use a crack shot at his side. This was the first time Brody had consulted with him on something of this nature, which made him feel good. Like he added value to the family other than being good with a gun.

Brody and Benjamin stomped around the back forty for

the rest of the day, trying in vain to pinpoint any of the land-marks depicted on the map. The dead tree on the map was long gone. Given that the river had changed course several times over the years since the map was sketched, they kept running into dead ends.

"It's like looking for a needle in a haystack," Ben said. "How does Percy do it? He didn't find the pearls when he was here before, but him and Henny have had lots of successes in their day."

"I guess it's in his blood," Brody said.

Eventually they lost the light and Brody signaled it was time to head back. Ben followed reluctantly. He really hated to be bested. Which served to strengthen his resolve when it came to Georgina. He couldn't let Philips waltz in here and pluck her out from under his nose. He needed to plan his next step.

"Thanks for your help, Ben," Brody said when they reached the ranch and saw to their horses.

"Don't know how much help I was," Ben mumbled.

"That just might be one of your problems," Brody said. "You underestimate your worth."

"I'm not feeling worth much these days," Ben admitted. "I thought I had an understanding with Georgina, but Philips is doing his best to cut me out. Can't say I blame her if she prefers his polished city ways to anything I have to offer."

"You and Georgina have been friends some time now, right?"

"I've known her a lot longer than he has."

"The way I see it, that gives you home advantage to the marshal."

"How so?"

"I've seen you at the card table a time or two. You never back down. You never fold."

"That's different."

"Not really. The way you're talking just now, sounds like you're throwing in your hand without any idea what the other man is bringing to the table. You think Georgina is worth fighting for?"

"She sure is," Ben said.

"It doesn't sound to me like much of a fight if you expected you'd just waltz right in there and declare your intentions, and have her fall in your lap."

Ben bristled. "I kinda thought, if two people agree they care for each other, it ought to be easy."

Brody clapped him on the shoulder. "You are dead wrong, my friend, if you think anything concerning the fairer sex is easy. Stack the deck, take the gloves off and get in there and prove to Georgina that's she's worth it."

Ben eyed Brody straight on. "She is worth it."

"Then that's something you need to prove to her. Because the one thing I know is that for most of her life, Georgina never felt she was worth much. It's up to you to go prove her wrong! To show her she's worth everything."

Benjamin grinned at Brody. "How'd you get so smart about women?"

"Believe me, I made my share of mistakes over the years with Laura. And I made a point to learn from each and every one of them what not to do next time."

Ben fell silent, digesting Brody's words as they left the barn.

"You want to come up to the house after? Grab a bite with Laura and I?"

That's all he needed! To spend his evening watching how the other half lived in their happy little family home.

The thought stopped him cold. Did he secretly hanker after what the others had? A wife? Children one day? He'd never thought that far ahead, other than him and Georgina ... Him and Georgina what?

"Not tonight, thanks," he said. "But maybe I could bring Georgina by some time. If things work out between us."

"Laura would love that. She's always liked Georgina. Ever since she helped her with the expansion at the café."

"Laura was involved with the changes at the cafe?"

Brody nodded. "She doesn't think I know anything, other than she's wealthy in her own right." He beamed proudly. "I have to hand it to her. Not only does she have some great ideas for this town, she has the means to help the other women and make them happen. Like the Women's Institute. And the hotel. Now she's all fired up with some scheme involving Hawkes's ranch house."

"And you don't mind?"

"Mind my wife being happy? Are you crazy? A happy wife makes for a happy life." He grinned as he said it. "Want some free advice? Figure out what Georgina needs to be happy. Help out where you can, but mostly let her think she managed it all on her own. The last thing these women of ours want is to feel dependent on a man."

"Truth?" Ben said. "I have a lot to learn."

Ben and Brody went their separate ways and Ben was crossing the yard to the ranch house when he ran into Blake.

"Got a few minutes?" Blake asked. "I could use a hand."

"Sure." Ben followed Blake to the workshop built on the back of the barn. "What with?"

"Something I got going. I need an extra set of hands."

Ben knew Blake was always tinkering with mechanical things, taking someone else's invention and trying to improve it. It sure wasn't something he was any good at.

Inside the workshop, Blake lit the lantern on the work-bench. "Can you shine this over here?"

When light illuminated the indicated area, Ben saw dozens of bits and pieces scattered across the work bench. "Isn't that the picture-taking camera that Henny brought back when her and Braydon were on their honeymoon?"

"Are you kidding? Henny would kill me if I took her precious camera apart," Blake said. "Braydon brought a different one back for me. Folks might think I'm crazy, but it occurred to me I might be able to modify the mechanism so it takes not only still pictures, but pictures that move."

"Sounds like a tall order," Benjamin said. "I know you made Storm a special sewing machine and all, but a camera that takes moving pictures?"

"Mark my words," Blake said. "If I don't figure out how to make it happen, someone else will."

Benjamin admired Blake's concentration as the other man combed through a pile of parts that, to him, looked like discarded junk. Some pieces he set aside into a separate pile, and others he tossed back into the fray. Faced with such a jumbled mish-mash, Benjamin wouldn't have a clue where to even start, but slowly and surely, with Benjamin holding pieces in place as instructed, Blake reassembled a goodly number of the parts into a cohesive unit.

Finally, Blake heaved a sigh and put down his tools. "That's good for now. Thanks, Ben."

"Anytime," Benjamin said. "Can I ask you something?"

"Sure thing," Blake said, as he wiped grease from his hands on a dirty-looking rag.

"How did you get Storm to let you know what she wanted? Like the scissors and the sewing machine you made special for her."

"She didn't tell me. I don't think she knew herself. I just

wanted to make her life easier, is all. Help make things better."

"Is that the reason you went chasing off to Colorado?"

Blake nodded. "Storm would never have been happy until she knew for sure what happened to the miserable cur she'd been married to."

"What if you'd got there and found out the man was still alive? That Storm was still his wife."

Blake leveled him with a long, intent look. "I would have done whatever it took to make sure Storm could be happy. Including kill the son of a bitch."

IN THE SAME way that Blake had wanted what was best for Storm, Benjamin wanted what was best for Georgina. And even though it was the hardest thing he had ever done, he forced himself to stay out of Bullet and away from her.

If Georgina chose to spend time with the marshal, maybe that was for the best. Maybe Philips was the one to make Georgina happy. Benjamin wanted Georgina to be happy more than anything, and if her happiness came about because of someone else, well it wasn't his place to get in the way.

He still couldn't fathom how Blake had known instinctively what it took for Storm to be happy. How had Bradley figured things out when it came to Amanda? How had Brody for Laura? The twins with their wives, or Braydon and Henrietta.

"You need to listen," they all told him. "Not to what she says, but what she doesn't say."

Their words left Benjamin more befuddled than ever. Hadn't he and Georgina always talked about everything under the sun? How was he supposed to figure out what she didn't say during those many conversations?

GEORGINA LOOKED up to see Lily and Rose rush into the café, chatting and laughing together in an animated fashion. She smiled to herself, comparing the difference to when she had first met Rose, quiet and thoughtful, yet determined to find her sister, who had been kidnapped. So determined Rose had somehow coerced the twins into helping her.

Georgina didn't know the whole story of how Rose got the twins to agree, but the three of them had successfully hunted down Lily and brought her safely to Bullet. Lily had lost her memory along with her ability to speak and didn't even know her own sister.

Now look at them! Bullet, a town that started out a lawless killing spot, had a healing effect on people these days.

"We have a surprise," Lily said.

"We need you to come with us," Rose said. "The other wives are meeting us over at the park."

Just the wives!

For a moment there, she had hoped the sisters meant the Mason brothers would be on hand as well. Benjamin had been doing his typical, make-himself-scarce routine since the day he had brought her flowers and learned she was going to a play with the marshal later that evening.

Maybe she oughtn't have followed Henrietta's advice, to make herself less available to Benjamin. Benjamin was different from Braydon, from all the Mason men, really, and although she longed to ask Lily and Rose if they'd seen him lately, she forced herself to keep quiet.

As the three of them reached the park, Georgina saw the other wives were waiting near the gazebo. Laura and Amanda had their little ones.

"It's over this way," Lily said as they reached the others.

"Closer to the river," Rose added.

It seemed to Georgina that the other ladies were as much in the dark as she was. Obediently, everyone fell into line and followed the sisters past the groomed area of the park toward the river, where the vegetation was more overgrown.

"Have you seen Benjamin lately?" Storm asked her as they filed along behind the others.

Georgina shook her head. "I guess he came to his senses and realized I wasn't the one for him after all."

Storm squeezed her arm. "When Blake found out I was already married, it didn't lessen his intentions one bit, and that was a far bigger stumbling block than you having a few dates with the marshal."

"Here we are. It starts here," Rose and Lily said. Both of them dropped to their knees as they spoke, and the other women gathered around them.

"What starts here?" Georgina asked Storm. She couldn't see over the heads of the others.

"No idea."

Georgina looked to the other women, who stood in a loose circle around the sisters, but they all seemed to be as in the dark as she was.

"Everyone in town has been so warm and welcoming to us," Lily said, as she smiled up at the other five women.

"We wanted to do something special as a thank-you," Rose said.

"We couldn't build a hotel or a hall," Lily joked. "Those things have already been done."

"The one thing we used to do away from our camp, something no one knew about but us, was to create these miniature magic fairy lands where we could play and imagine a better life than the one we had."

"So we decided to build a miniature magic fairy land here, near the park, for everyone to enjoy. It's not quite finished," Lily said. "But we hoped if we showed you what we had been doing, you might all help us. We don't have any paint, and we need some signs and a few other things before it's done."

Georgina edged closer, and then she saw it. The little scene spread in all directions, depicting tiny houses, cobblestone streets, stores and wooden sidewalks. There was even a church with a cemetery behind it with tiny rocks for headstones. The township turned into a miniature trail through the thicket, where the sisters had created a ranch with perfectly proportioned animals, and a miniature well built from tiny pebbles.

"We thought we might put up some little fences so it doesn't accidentally get trampled," Rose said. "That way everyone can discover it and enjoy it."

Lily sat back on her heels and smiled at the group as a whole. "Storm, you must have wondered what we were doing with all your fabric scraps. We used them to make a whole lot of tiny rag doll people that the children in town can bring here. That way they can let their imaginations roam in the miniature land we made."

"We thought Laura could take some of the rag dolls to the school and give them to the new teacher to distribute," Rose added.

"And Georgina and Henrietta could pass them out to families with children when they're at the café or the hotel. Maybe as a reward for good manners," Lily said.

"And Storm, you could give them to the children at the library," Rose added.

"Well?" The two sisters faced them. "What do you think?"

Laura turned to the other women. "I think we're an amazing group of highly talented individuals and I'm proud to call you all my sisters."

Georgina burst into applause. The others joined in. Before Georgina knew it, they were all on their hands and knees exclaiming over the intricate details of the scene before them.

"I wish I'd had something like this to play with when I was young," Henrietta said. "But my brothers would have trashed it."

"It's enchanting," Georgina said.

"That's what we'll call it," Lily said. "The Enchanted Land."

"We'll tell the youngsters in town that it belongs to all of them," Laura said. "And none of them would dare to damage it in any way."

Storm nodded. "Well, tell them it's guarded by a magical creature who's here to keep it safe."

Georgina didn't know much about youngsters, but she had a feeling if they all took an interest in the Enchanted Land, that it would, indeed, remain safe from harm.

"HEY BENJAMIN!" Ben heard Storm call him as she drove the carriage down the driveway and stopped. "Blake told me you're trying to figure out what Georgina wants."

Blake and his big mouth!

"Well, not really. Kind of," he muttered, staring at some spot off in the distance.

"This may or may not help," Storm said. "But she's been borrowing books from the library about other places."

"What kind of other places?"

"Cities out east. Books that explain what it's like in New York and Boston."

His gut tightened. "You think maybe she's fixing to move?" Georgina had changed her mind about Seattle, but there was a whole other rest of the world out there.

"Not that she's mentioned. But I thought it might be helpful for you to know that."

"Thanks, Storm. I appreciate it." Ben started to ride off, when he heard Storm call him back a second time. "You should talk to Henrietta. I understand Georgina's been spending a fair amount of time at the hotel. Henny might know something that would be helpful."

Ben stared at her. "I thought you ladies always stuck together. Why are you telling me this?"

"Silly, Ben. We want Georgina to be happy, is all."

So did he. "What makes you think I'm the one who can make her happy?"

Storm looked at him and gave her head a disbelieving shake, as if he was a totally dense creature, which maybe he was. "What if I told you Marshal Philips hasn't been around lately?"

"He hasn't! How do you know?"

"He stopped by the ranch before he left. Put in his bid for Brody to become mayor."

The words had barely left her mouth before Benjamin wheeled his horse in a circle and started off down the driveway.

"Where are you going?" she called after him.

"I have to go see Georgina."

He made it to town in record time, only to find that Georgina wasn't at her house or the café. The library was closed, so he stopped in at the hotel where he sought out Henrietta.

"Any idea where I might find Georgina?"

"What day is it?"

Benjamin shrugged. Days of the week had stopped being important to him a long time ago.

Henrietta cocked her head thoughtfully. "It's Tuesday. That means she's gone to visit old Mrs. Hemshaw on the far side of town."

This was the first Benjamin had heard of such a thing. "What's she doing there?"

"Mrs. Hemshaw was a friend of her mother. She's quite elderly and doesn't get around very well these days. Georgina goes by every few days to take her food and books and anything else she might need. She makes sure the old lady has candles and kerosene, and sees to anything else that might need doing."

"I never knew Georgina did that," Benjamin said. "I would have helped her."

Henrietta gave him a telling look. "Did you ever think, these are the kinds of things you ought to know about Georgina's life? The way she's always putting others first?"

"You're right," Benjamin said. "She was always such a good listener, I never learned much out about her."

"I'm betting it wouldn't go amiss should you show up at Mrs. Hemshaw's all concerned and interested," Henrietta said. "Do you know which house it is?"

"I'll find it," Benjamin said.

"Invite Georgina to the ranch for Valentine's Day," Henrietta said, as he prepared to leave. "It's Bradley and

Amanda's first wedding anniversary and they're throwing a small party. You do know what Valentine's Day is don't you, Ben?"

"Not really."

Henrietta made a tsk-tsk sound. "I suggest you get yourself to the library and read up on it. That is, if you're of a mind to do some proper wooing."

Ben left more confused than ever. Henny had told him to read up on Valentine's Day. Blake had told him to find out what would make Georgina happy. And he had no idea how to go about any of it.

He was still pondering the challenge as he made his way to Mrs. Hemshaw's farm. He thought he knew the place, but it turned out he was mistaken, and he ended up on a dead-end driveway that led nowhere.

He had barely got turned around and back onto the main road toward Yuma when he spotted Georgina's carriage stopped on the road up ahead. An unsavory character on a sad-looking horse was blocking her way. The man had a gun pointed at Georgina.

CHAPTER 9

"Kindly move out of my way. I have nothing for you." Georgina didn't take her eyes off the mangy-looking man who had accosted her on the road back to town.

"What do you mean? You gotta have something of value."

"I mean you picked the wrong person to rob." Georgina was relieved her voice didn't tremble, for the rest of her certainly was. She'd stayed later than she intended visiting her old friend, and the light was starting to fade, but she could still see the mean expression on the face of the man before her. She had already judged her chance of driving past him before he got off a shot as not very good odds.

"I guess we'll just see about that." He kneed his horse closer to the carriage, and his bloodshot eyes roved over her bosom. "You might not have any baubles, but I bet you have something old Hank would like."

She could smell him from here, and despite the urge to bolt, Georgina forced herself to sit completely still when the stranger reached a dirty hand toward her.

Never show fear!

It was a message drummed into her from an early age.

"Let's get a better look at you, girlie." The stranger's evil smiled displayed a few broken, yellow teeth with gaps between.

She flinched when he raised his gun toward her and used the barrel to tip her hat from her head. Her headwear glanced off the side of the carriage and rolled into the dust.

Georgina's heart raced. Her mouth felt dry.

"Little longer in the tooth than I first thought," the man said. "Still, can't much tell the difference in the dark."

When he leaned toward her, she shuddered as his foul breath hit her full in the face. Before he got close enough to touch her, a shot rang out. Her would-be-attacker jerked. Seconds later, he pitched head first from his horse and into the dirt road. The would-be robber's sorry nag didn't move, but Georgina's horse gave a nervous snort and side-stepped, jostling the carriage.

Heart in her throat, she looked up to see Benjamin hurtling toward her, anger and concern on his face. He reined his horse to a stop inches from her carriage.

"Are you all right? Did he hurt you?"

She glanced from Benjamin to where the unmoving man lay in the road with a gaping wound in his head, then back to Benjamin. "You killed him."

"I'd do that and worse to anyone who dared try to hurt you," Benjamin said as he re-holstered his gun. He ran the back of his hand across her cheek. "If he harmed one hair on your head—"

She raised a trembling hand to the base of her throat. "I can't believe you killed him."

He caught her hand in both of his and raised it to his lips. "I'm just glad you're all right. That I got here in time."

In spite of herself, Georgina felt her eyes start to fill. She began to shake. Unbidden, a sob escaped from her throat, followed by a second.

In seconds, Benjamin was beside her in the carriage, taking her in his arms. He held her as if he'd been doing it all her life. Smoothing her hair. Rubbing her back. Letting her cry. Because once she started, she couldn't seem to stop.

Caught and held against him, absorbing his strength and the warmth of his body against hers, Georgina felt as if she'd finally come home. A safe place where she was protected and cherished. A place she never wanted to leave.

Eventually, her sobs slowed, then stopped altogether, but she couldn't bring herself to leave Benjamin's arms. "I'm sorry," she said. "I never cry."

He tipped her face up toward his and gently wiped her damp cheek with the pad of one thumb. "You can cry whenever you want, baby. I'll always be here to wipe your tears."

His words set off a fresh torrent of weeping. She wasn't alone!

Darkness fell as Benjamin held her and reassured her. As the minutes passed, something inside her, something that had been walled off and isolated her whole life, slowly unfurled and came to life.

When she raised her face to his, he kissed her brow, softly, reassuringly, lovingly.

"You're in shock," he said. "It's good to get it out."

"I suddenly feel so light," she said, wonderingly. "Like everything I've held in and repressed my entire life has just broken free and floated away."

"I want you to always feel that way," he said huskily as he smoothed her hair and pressed a kiss to the top of her head. "I promise I'll do everything I can to help make it happen."

She rested her head against his shoulder. "What will

happen to that horrid man? And don't tell me you'll leave him here for the coyotes."

"Tempting," Benjamin said. "I guess we'll take his body into town. Wait for the law to come by and deal with things."

She lifted her head and looked into his eyes. "Brody wants you to run for sheriff. You'd be good at it."

"I dunno," he said. "I'm good at the killing part. Not so sure about the lawmaking part."

"Despite what you might say, I know you don't relish taking a life. You let that other man go, the one who showed up looking for you at the café that night."

Benjamin shrugged. "That was different. He was only after *me*. If he'd come after you, it'd be a different story."

She inched away from his side before she got too comfortable being in his arms. "You're a fair man, Benjamin. You'd make a wonderful sheriff."

He waved her words away. "Never mind me. I'm proud of *you*. The way you stood up to this vermin, so brave and strong."

She glanced down at her lap. She wasn't used to talking about herself, never mind hearing admiration steered her way. "Nothing new there. I've always had to be strong."

"Not anymore," he said. "Not now you've got me."

But did she? Did she really?

"How did you know where I was?"

"I missed you," he said simply. "I realized I was a fool to step back and see if Philips was the one who could truly make you happy."

She shook her head. Dear, sweet Benjamin! "Did you even hear me that night we shared such a passionate kiss? When I said you were the one who had claimed my heart?"

"I guess, when you stepped out with Philips the next

night, I thought it was just something you said in the heat of the moment. Something you didn't mean."

She shook her head. Even when men appeared to be listening, it was clear they weren't *really* listening.

"I was happy to see you come along tonight, but I hope this one incident doesn't mean you expect me to turn into a fainting pansy. Some weak, lily-livered, pathetic excuse for a woman."

He hugged her close. "Not for one second. But I think, together, we can help each other be the best people we can."

His lips found hers in a kiss full of hope. Full of promise. Full of commitment. Full of love.

As their mouths mated, she felt a wellspring of emotion inside her bubble up and start to overflow. As if the tears and sorrow she spent earlier had made room for something better. Something far more powerful and fulfilling.

She was finally complete.

They hauled Georgina's attacker to Bullet on the back of his tired old nag, Benjamin holding the reins of the other horse, along with his own. Already Georgina missed the warmth of his body alongside hers, but he rode close to her carriage, and every time she glanced over at him, he met her look with a reassuring smile that made her tingle clear down to her toes.

When they reached her house, he followed her around back and took over the task of unhitching and brushing her horse.

"Any idea when Philips plans to be back this way?" he asked.

Georgina shook her head.

"In that case, I guess I'll take our friend here out to the ranch. Save the sheriff in Yuma the paperwork. His won't be the first nameless body buried out in the desert." He gave her a stern look. "And no more going off by yourself like that again."

When she opened her mouth in protest, he silenced her with a kiss. "You don't see any of the wives trotting out into the wilderness by themselves, do you? The town, the entire territory, is growing and changing. I hate to think what might have happened if I hadn't come along."

"All the more reason for you to become sheriff," she said, primly, secretly thrilled by his possessive manner. "Bring some law and order back into these parts so it's safe for normal folk."

"I'll take that under advisement," he said, trailing one hand from her ear to her cheek and down the side of her neck. Shivers of awareness shot through her at his touch. "Turns out there's a party at the ranch next week. Amanda and Bradley's wedding anniversary is on Valentine's Day."

"So it is," Georgina said. "It's hard to believe it's been a whole year since they were married."

"Anyway, I'll come get you. I don't want you driving out there by yourself."

"To the ranch?" she said. "Now you're being just plain silly. I've made that trip alone more times than I can count."

"Not anymore," he said stubbornly. "This time you're going with me."

Just the way he said it, all masterful and possessive gave her a tingle of excitement.

"And no more gadding about on your own," he added as he mounted his horse and looped the second horse's reins around his wrist.

She followed him to the street and watched him as long as she could see him, thrilled when he turned and waved just before he vanished from sight. Hugging herself in disbelief, she scampered inside.

THE RANCH HOUSE was lit up like the new year's fireworks, light blazing from every window on the lower floor. Not long ago, Benjamin would have worried it meant something bad had happened, but since the day they took down Hawkes, he'd felt a sense of calm settle over the ranch and the countryside.

Inside, the whole family, little ones and all, were in attendance. "Glad you're back," Barron said.

"Yes, indeed," said Lily. "We were just talking about getting into the old habit of having big family dinners here at the house again."

"If we can convince Brody to clear out all his stuff," Laura said in a teasing way. "No one seems to understand why he needs to spread his precious papers between two houses when one house seems adequate for everyone else."

She jiggled little Charlotte on her knee. The girl was determinedly reaching across the table toward a coffee cup safely out of reach, short, dimpled fingers splayed, grunting with the effort. Ben figured Brody would have his hands more than full in no time.

"I'm sure Ben would love to not have his home invaded at all hours," added Amanda.

Ben shrugged and pulled a chair up around the table where the others either sat or stood. "Kinda got used to it. What's going on?"

"We're trying to come up with a name for Hawkes's ranch," Braydon said. "We don't want locals referring to it as the "old Hawkes place" into the next century. We want that name wiped off the history books."

"It needs a new identity," Henrietta said. She snapped

her fingers. "What about Dove House? A dove is still a bird, but it's a beautiful, gentle bird that symbolizes peace."

"The dove is mentioned all through the Bible," Rose added.

"And have you seen pictures of some of the ancient goddesses?" Storm added. "They're often depicted holding a dove."

"That's ideal!" Laura said. "Dove House suits its new purpose perfectly."

Ben glanced from one to the other of his family members. "I came in late on the conversation. Have you all got something in mind for the ranch house?"

Brody rolled his eyes in a good-natured way. "The ladies have. And there's not a man in this room foolish enough to try and stop them once they have an idea in their heads."

Laura gave his arm a playful slap with her free hand. "A wise decision."

"Is someone going to fill me in?" Benjamin asked.

"Storm had the idea originally," Amanda said.

"The rest of us thought it was perfect," Henrietta added.

"And Lily and Rose are taking it on as their own special project," Storm said. "Now that their other project is all finished."

"Other project?" Ben asked suspiciously, remembering the furtive comings and goings of the sisters.

"They created something wonderful at the park," Amanda said. "Something the whole town can enjoy."

Before Ben could ask what the "something wonderful" was, the conversation resumed.

"We know the rest of you are busy," Rose said. "And Lily and I really want to be involved in this new project."

"Particularly something of this nature and importance," Lily added. "A way to help other women escape from a bad situation." The two sisters looked at each other and nodded emphatically.

When little Samuel let out a fretful wail, Amanda opened the front of her blouse and stuffed a boob in his mouth, all without missing a beat.

Ben blanched and looked away. No one else around the table seemed to have noticed. If they did, it was apparently nothing they hadn't seen before.

"I'm still in the dark," he said. "What are these plans for the old Hawkes—I mean Dove House?"

"Dove House will be set up as a safe, temporary home for women and children who need to escape from a bad home life like the one I had," Storm said.

Ben's gaze roved from face to face, aware most of them had been in a difficult situation at one point or another in their earlier lives. Brody had provided a safe haven for the men when they were younger, but a woman like Storm, all alone in the world, didn't have much choice other than put up with her situation.

"Did you invite Georgina to the party?" Amanda asked.

Her blouse was once more buttoned and the baby laid over her shoulder. As she patted the little one's back, Benjamin heard a hearty burp that sounded far too loud to have come from such a small person

"I did," Benjamin said. He snapped his fingers. "I almost forgot. Got me a dead body out front. Hoping I can get a hand burying it tomorrow."

As they all clamored in at once, wanting to know what happened, Benjamin realized just how much he enjoyed being part of the family. And how much better it would be to have Georgina here as well.

He caught Brody's eye across the room. "Did you tell Kennedy yet whether or not you decided to run for mayor?"

"The twins are champing at the bit to oversee the mining operation. Once it's up and running, I kind of got the hint they don't want me in the way." Brody grinned as he spoke. "Now that Braydon's not dancing to Henrietta's beck and call,"—he ducked good-naturedly when Braydon pretended to throw a punch his way— "the rest of you can handle the ranch. I don't expect mayoring to be a full-time job anyway."

Benjamin addressed his brothers. "Think the rest of you can manage without me around here every day? Strikes me as Bullet needs someone to uphold the law around here and send any unsavory types packing."

The room filled with whoops and cheers. The wives looked on smiling in approval. An inner warmth spread through Benjamin, a slow uncurling sensation from the top down, as if his feet were finally putting down roots in this sandy Arizona soil.

NOBODY WAS around when Benjamin saddled up early the next morning and headed over to where the survey crew had been set up. Brody had said the men had packed up and left, but Benjamin wanted to check and see for himself. Something about the two he had seen off on their own last time he was there had been nagging at him ever since.

Not only did the pair appear to have their own agenda, he'd overheard them mention the old gang from these parts. Benjamin wasn't about to sit back and let anything or anyone jeopardize this new life he was creating for himself and the people he cared about.

It was just past dawn when he reached the spot the surveyors had used as their base. Sure enough, all the men, tents and equipment were gone. The only evidence of them being there at all was a bunch of tracks in the sandy ground, hooves and scrape marks where something heavy must have been dragged.

Benjamin got down for a closer look. He circled the site slowly. When he reached the far side, he stopped and squatted, studying the tracks up close. Once again, his instincts hadn't let him down. The ground showed clear signs that two horses had taken off in a different direction from the rest of the party. He straightened and stared off the way the pair had headed. Straight toward Copper Moon.

He returned to his horse and mounted up. There was no time like the present to put on his lawman hat and find out what was going on.

CHAPTER 10

The two riders had a head start, but Benjamin had the advantage of knowing the area and not having his mount weighted down with gear. Even when he lost the trail over the rockier spots of the landscape, it was easy to pick up again. The duo were making no effort to cover their tracks, and it was pretty clear they had a specific destination in mind. Being a betting man, he'd put his money on them making a beeline for the caves.

He hated being wrong. But this time he was, as he found out hours later when he caught sight of his quarry up ahead. Their horses stood off to one side while straight ahead, shovels in hand, the pair were busy digging.

The ground was soft and they had made a fair bit of progress, both standing nearly waist-deep in a large hole. Benjamin dismounted and continued forward on foot, using whatever he could find for cover.

He needn't have bothered, for they were too busy arguing to look around or pay attention to what was happening nearby.

"Shouldn't we have found it by now?" whined the skinny one as he straightened up and leaned on his shovel.

"Shut up and keep digging," said the burlier of the two. "I was here with Hawkes when he followed the map and marked it off."

"If'n he was so sure this is where loot was buried, why didn't he come get it for himself?"

"This is Copper Moon land. He wanted to wait till he had the property deed all tied up nice and proper in his name."

"Hawkes was getting soft in the head," scoffed the skinny one. "He never used to care about stuff like that."

"You might be right about that. Made a bigger fool of himself with all that wedding nonsense at the ranch. Never even saw the trap, even after he strolled right into it."

Silence ensued as the pair resumed their digging. Benjamin approached stealthily till he was right at the edge of the hole.

"You boys are trespassing," he said quietly, rifle in hand as he looked down on the duo.

It was almost comical the way the two started, panicked and fell all over each other in an attempt to get away, only to find there was no place for them to go. The sides of the hole they'd dug were soft, and every step in the sandy soil sent them sliding back down to the bottom.

The fat one, clearly the leader, was sweating profusely. "How about we make you all a deal?"

"What kind of a deal?" Benjamin asked.

"We cut you in on what we find here."

Benjamin pretended to consider the offer. "How much?"

Fatso licked his lips. "Say, ten percent?"

Benjamin laughed and cocked his rifle. "Don't insult me."

"Twenty, then," said the man. "Twenty-five, even. That's a more than generous offer when we done all the work."

Benjamin raised his rifle and took aim. "I've got six brothers I'd need to share it with. That doesn't leave a very big portion for any of us compared to what the two of you would walk away with."

"Hey, mister," piped up the skinny one. "They don't need to know. We wouldn't be saying nothing about it, would we?" He glanced to his partner for confirmation.

Tubs just nodded, eyes narrowed, as he watched Benjamin from beneath half-closed lids. The second he moved, Benjamin shot him in the hand going for his gun. The man let out a yelp of pain. Blood gushed from his wound.

The skinny one's eyes grew round as saucers. "How about you take it all? Everything we find is yours."

"That's a little better offer," Benjamin said. "Unfortunately, your buddy here won't be able to pull his weight with the digging now that I've shot him. That means you'd have to do all the work."

"I don't mind. I'm a hard worker. I can—"

"Well, well now! What have we here?"

Benjamin didn't need to turn around to know his brothers had ridden up behind him. He'd heard their horses when they were a fair distance off. He kept a watchful eye on the two before him as saddle leather creaked behind him as the others dismounted.

Bradley reached his side first. "Whatcha got here, Ben?"

"Got me a couple of rats trapped in a hole. At least that's what it looks like."

One by one, the other brothers joined Benjamin and Bradley to stand, shoulder to shoulder.

"Rats for sure," Bradley said.

"Rats that did Hawkes's dirty work," Benjamin said.

"You know it," Bradley said. He addressed the men who stood below, staring up with loathing in their eyes. "You two know anything about setting dynamite? Cause someone laid a booby trap on the ranch a while back. Easily could have left me badly maimed, if not blown to kingdom come."

"We was just learning," bragged the fat one.

"You must have got a little better with dynamite by the time you blew up Amanda's house," Blake said in conversational tones. "Not caring whether or not our women were inside."

"Yeah, we'd had a little more practice by then," slim said.

"Know anything about poisoning a ranch's well?" Brody asked pleasantly. "Cause that little piece of business could have left a whole lot of people real sick. Maybe even dead."

"Caught grief from Hawkes over that one," said the fat one, pointing to his partner. "This idiot poisoned the wrong well."

"How was I to know?" whined the other man.

"And you're the ones who set the dynamite at the park the day I was getting married." Braydon said. "It wasn't much of a wedding gift."

"Never mind that. He's the one you want," said the skinny one, indicating the fat one. "He's the one who set up Joe the night Hawkes killed him."

"Is that right?" Bishop said. "Wish we'd known that all those times Barron and I saw you when we were watching Hawkes's place."

"Both looked to be real chummy with Hawkes," Barron agreed. "Wonder what other deeds they were responsible for? Probably too many to count."

"Storm saw the men who set the fire at the Institute Hall

when it was just started getting built. She'd know for sure if it was these two or not," Blake said.

"What if it was?" blustered the fat one, cradling his injured hand. "You boys aren't about to shoot us down in cold blood."

"I wouldn't be so sure about that," Brody said. "Anything else you'd like to confess to while you have our undivided attention?"

"Saving it for the magistrate," chubs said cockily.

"In that case ..."

Benjamin raised his rifle at the same time as the others. Seven shots rang simultaneously through the countryside. The two men landed on their backs in the hole, staring up sightlessly.

"I could have taken care of them myself," Benjamin said, lowering his rifle.

"Can't be doing much of that once you're a lawman," Brody said. "Besides, we're a family. In this together."

"Nice of them to dig us this big hole," Braydon said. "Saved us a lot of work."

Brody nodded. "Let's get them buried. Too bad we didn't get the chance to tell them Hawkes pinpointed this spot from a phony map Amanda planted to replace the real one."

"You really think there's loot from Red's Rowdies stashed someplace on the ranch?" Benjamin asked. "You and I didn't have any luck when we were out looking."

"I'd say there's a fifty-fifty chance it was a tale concocted by Hawkes to justify killing the members of his gang," Brody said. "Even if there were valuables hidden on the ranch, they don't belong to us. The most valuable treasure on this ranch is that it brought us together to form a family."

~

GEORGINA OUGHT TO FEEL HAPPIER. At long last, her beloved town was free from the unsavory influence of Hawkes and his henchmen. Thanks to the influx of visitors to the area, the café had never been busier and was turning a tidy profit.

Ever since the night she was attacked, Benjamin had shown up each evening as she closed the café to escort her on an outing or simply sit by her side on the big old porch swing, drinking sweet tea and talking the way they used to.

"You seem restless, my love," he said, one particularly warm evening when she found herself unable to sit still.

Turning to face him, she saw herself mirrored in his sincere gaze. "I didn't know it was that obvious."

"It is to someone who knows you as well as I do."

His words struck a chord. He *did* know her better than anyone else.

She heaved a sigh. "Don't take this the wrong way. I'm happy spending time with you each evening."

"And yet—"

"I don't want to spend the rest of my life at the café. Something I only realized when that Mexican couple offered to buy it. But I can't, I won't just close it down. And there's no one in town in a position to buy it."

Benjamin fell quiet, obviously deep in thought. "I'd offer to help you with it," he said finally. "But I promised Brody I'll run for sheriff."

"Oh, no," she said. "I didn't mean that at all. Being sheriff is a far better use of your talents. And I have a capable staff. I just look at my friends. Henrietta has the hotel. Storm has her seamstress work and the book wagon. Amanda created the Women's Institute hall, which has made a huge difference to this town. And you can see Laura's magic touch everywhere you look. Did you know she offered to teach any children who come to stay at Dove

House? Even Lily and Rose have a dream to follow. And here I sit, doing the exact same thing I've done my entire life."

She laid a finger on his lips when he started to open his mouth. "And don't reassure me there's value in what I'm doing. I'm well aware of that. But you asked why I'm restless." She forced a laugh. "A much longer answer than you were expecting, I'm sure."

He kissed her fingertips before he gently removed her hand, keeping it clasped warmly within his. "That isn't what I was about to say, although it's certainly true. I was about to suggest that you approach your staff and offer them a chance to become partners in the café."

"Partners?" she asked.

"Brody did something similar with the ranch. Each of us owns a chunk of it, with money taken over time from our wages. It gives us pride of ownership and a reason to work our butts off so we all reap the benefits. No one would dare to slack off."

"How will that work if Brody becomes mayor, with you as sheriff?"

"Brody's figuring out those details. But I bet a similar arrangement could work with the café. Instead of you carrying all the weight and responsibility, it gets distributed among everyone there."

"That's an interesting suggestion," Georgina said, laying her head on his shoulder. "I'll give it some thought."

They rocked in comfortable silence for several moments.

Like an old married couple, Georgina thought. Except there had been no talk of marriage. Perhaps Benjamin was content the way things were. Old Mrs. Hemshaw had long been widowed, after which she had spent many happy times with a gentleman caller before he, too, passed on. Georgina had asked her once why the two of them had never gotten married.

Mrs. Hemshaw had laughed and told her marriage was designed to make the husband's life more comfortable, rather than the wife's. Having nursed one husband through his illness, the old lady had no desire to ever do so again. Georgina saw a fair amount of truth in her old friend's words. But when she saw Amanda and Laura with their babes— She sighed.

Abruptly, Benjamin stiffened and sat bolt upright.

"What?" she asked.

"Horses approaching," he said, his hand hovering near his holster. He relaxed when the riders came into view.

Georgina rose to greet the newcomers, thinking how nice it was to have a man around. Especially a man like Benjamin, who was capable of dealing with pretty much anything.

"I hope we're not intruding," Henrietta said as she dismounted, closely followed by Braydon. Henrietta wore the man-style trousers that had shocked the town when she first arrived.

When she noticed Georgina's scrutiny, Henrietta laughed. "They're so much more comfortable for riding. I know, as proprietress of the hotel, I ought to appear more respectable, but I hope people will indulge me."

Braydon gave her a loving kiss. "Old habits die hard, do they not?"

"Let me remind you who you fell in love with, my dear."

Braydon gazed down affectionately at his wife. "I've never forgotten. Nor have I ever tried to clip your wings."

Henrietta clapped him on the shoulder. "Smart man."

"Won't you please join us?" Belatedly, Georgina remembered her manners and indicated the two comfy wicker chairs on the porch. "Can I offer you some tea?"

"Nothing for me, thanks," Henrietta said.

"Me either," Braydon said. "Ben, can I have a word?"

"Sure thing." Ben rose, gave Georgina a quick kiss on her forehead and followed Braydon over toward the horses.

Henrietta gave Georgina a happy smile. "I was going to wait to talk to you tomorrow at the party, but—" she shrugged. "You know how it is when we all get together. It's craziness. This seemed a better idea. Just the two of us."

Georgina straightened. "Is something wrong?"

"Not at all. Quite the opposite. The hotel has barely been open six weeks and it's already busier than I anticipated."

"That's a good thing, right?"

"In many ways," Henrietta agreed. "The truth is, it's quickly becoming more than I can handle. Braydon has been wonderful, but I know him. He's itching to be back getting his hands dirty on the ranch. And much as I love him, I don't want to be tethered to him twenty-four hours a day."

"I'm not sure—"

"I need a right hand," Henrietta said. "I need someone who can guide the hotel and the staff with a firm, yet experienced hand when I'm not there. I also want someone who would be willing to travel back East if required, maybe with me, maybe alone, to help promote not just the hotel, but the entire area. As rail travel becomes more accessible, predictions are for an influx of visitors to Arizona."

"I heard that, also," Georgina said.

"I know you have the café, but I also know you were willing to sell it not long ago, looking to make a change. With you and Ben making a match of it, it seems unlikely you have any plans to move, but perhaps the hotel is a change you might consider. Just think about it," she said. "No need to decide in any sort of a hurry."

"I will consider it," Georgina said. "And I appreciate your faith in me. As for Ben and I—" She glanced to where the two men stood near the horses, deep in conversation.

"The Mason men are all a little slow on the uptake," Henrietta said. "He'll come around in his own time, same as the rest of them."

"I'm not sure that's what I want," Georgina said. She leaned toward her friend and lowered her voice. "How did you know for sure? About Braydon being the one, I mean?"

Henrietta pressed her lips together thoughtfully. "I'd have to say, it was when I realized that he knew me better than I knew myself. Accepting that was scary and exhilarating at the same time. But it felt right." She paused. "It's like, if I'm thinking about a song and I hear the tune in my head but can't remember the words, and suddenly he just starts singing it out loud."

Georgina's eyes widened. "That sounds terribly romantic."

"It needn't always be romantic." Henrietta pressed the tips of her fingers together. "It's like that night you were attacked. Somehow Ben knew he needed to find you. No other reason than he knew, deep in his heart and soul, that you needed him. And there he was."

"And there he still is," Georgina said, looking again to where Benjamin stood alongside Braydon. The two men could not be any more different in temperament and upbringing, and yet there they stood, brothers in every way that mattered.

As she stared across the yard she realized, in that

moment, that she loved Benjamin with every fiber of her being. And always would.

~

"WHAT DO YOU HAVE THERE?" Benjamin asked the next evening as he picked her up for the party at the ranch. She climbed into the carriage, clutching a small, covered basket in one hand.

"Just a little anniversary gift for the happy couple," she said.

If she felt disappointed when Benjamin hadn't shown up with a small nosegay of flowers or a special card for Valentine's Day, she squelched it, turning her thoughts to happier ones. It was a beautiful evening. One she would spend not only with Benjamin, but with all her friends. And while she might not be one of the brides, she had certainly been accepted into their fold.

"That was very thoughtful of you, my love." Guiding the reins with one hand, he reached across to capture both her hands, raising them to his lips before he turned admiring eyes her way. "You look exceptionally beautiful tonight."

"Thank you," she said, pleased that he had noticed the extra care she had taken with her appearance.

"I haven't seen that frock before. Is it new?"

"As a matter of fact, it is," she said, settling back. She hadn't known he paid a mind to what she wore.

"I was certainly a dense idiot to take so long to realize what you mean to me, and how wonderful life is when we're together."

"It is wonderful," she agreed.

"Do you mind about the party tonight?" he asked, his fingers still linked with hers. "I confess to selfishly having enjoyed our evenings together this past while, just the two of us."

"As have I. But tonight will be a nice change. I haven't seen everyone all together since Barron and Lily's wedding."

"The whole gang went all out for the party," Benjamin said. "Act surprised when you see."

She didn't have to act surprised. She'd never seen the ranch look quite so fancied up, not even when there had been a wedding taking place.

"Who all is expected?" she asked. "I thought it was just the family."

"And Percy," Benjamin said. "It started out to be a tea. Then Bradley and Blake decided fancy sandwiches and cakes were too sissy so they did up a barbecue with ribs and beans and cornbread and slaw."

"Everything smells delicious," Georgina said, as Benjamin parked the carriage and circled around to help her down.

"We won't be eating for a while," Benjamin said. "In the meantime, there's something I want to show you over this way."

"Let me just congratulate Amanda and Bradley first," Georgina said.

"They're over there on the porch."

Hand in hand, she and Benjamin crossed the yard to the ranch house where Amanda rocked a peacefully sleeping Samuel.

Georgina passed Amanda the gift basket. "I brought you an anniversary present," she said.

"That wasn't necessary," Amanda said. "But thank you all the same."

"I wanted to. I think today is a wonderful excuse for a celebration."

"Just you wait," Amanda said. "There will be lots more to celebrate later."

"What did Amanda mean by that?" Georgina asked Benjamin, once they were out of earshot. "Is one of the couples in the family way?"

"I don't know anything about that," Benjamin said.

As they crossed the yard, Georgina stopped to have a word with others they passed. At her side, Benjamin was certainly out of sorts, chafing with impatience each time they were approached by someone new. Eventually she put him out of his misery and let him drag her off to whatever he wanted to show her. On the way, she waved to Henrietta, who was deep in conversation with her old friend, Percy.

"What's Percy doing now that he's back?" Georgina asked. "Is he fixing to stay?"

"I'm not sure," Benjamin said. "You'll get a chance to ask him later. Over this way," he said, tugging at her hand.

"But I haven't said hello to the twins and their wives yet."

"There'll be time for that later."

"You're acting so mysterious," she said. "I thought this was supposed to be a party."

He blew out a breath. "I never knew you to be so ornery."

"And I never knew you to act like this before." Was it her imagination, or did he look nervous?

"I just really hope you like what I have to show you."

With one arm around her waist, he guided her past the six cabins that had been built on the slight rise behind the ranch house, one for each couple as they tied the knot. The ground was uneven and she stumbled once, but Ben kept firm hold.

"Would you kindly slow down?" she said. "I feel like you're dragging me."

"I'm sorry." He stopped. "I'm just a bit anxious is all. We're almost there."

She followed his gaze. Ahead, on the rise overlooking the river, a short distance from the cabins, sat a swing much like the one on her porch. She gave him a puzzled look. Who got this nervous about a swing?

"I was really enjoying our evenings lately on your porch swing. Did it a bit backwards, I guess. Built the swing before the porch. Come try it out."

He tugged her over to sit next to him, and with one push of his foot sent them into a slow rocking motion. "You like it?"

"It's a much better view than my swing," she said. "Not as rickety, either." She ran a hand along the wooden back. "You made this?"

"Mostly," he said. "Blake helped me with the moving parts."

"I like it." She looked back over her shoulder. "Now can we get back to the party?"

"In just a minute."

"You're perspiring." Georgina reached over and blotted at his forehead with her hankie. "I've never seen you like this before. Are you feeling all right? Maybe you have a fever."

"I've never been better," he said. "At least I will be in a minute." He cleared his throat again and reached into his inside pocket to pull out a lace-trimmed envelope. "Valentine's wouldn't be Valentine's if I didn't give my girl a fancy card."

Her first Valentine! Georgina was instantly ashamed of her earlier thoughts that Benjamin hadn't known the importance of the day.

"Thank you."

"I thought about making one, but then I saw this one over at the Yuma Mercantile and knew it was the one."

Georgina's mouth dropped as she opened the envelope and pulled out the card that was inside. The silver paper caught the sunlight and reflected it back to her. "I've never seen anything so fancy." She opened the card to find that along with the rhyming verse and Benjamin's signature was a paper hand.

She turned to him. "The card is beautiful. I'm afraid I'm not sure about the significance of the hand."

Benjamin nodded. "I didn't know either. I did some reading and found out it's a way for me to ask formally for permission to court you. I wish I'd known about it sooner. I could have done things right, way back at the start."

She leaned forward to kiss him. "You're doing things right now."

"There's more." From his vest pocket he pulled out a pair of ladies' gloves and passed them to her.

"Gloves," she said, turning them over. "What a thoughtful gift." They were the texture and color of freshly churned butter.

"Wait," he said, when she went to slip one hand inside.

"Don't tell me there's more?" she joked. "I didn't get you a thing."

"Tradition is, if a man gives a lady a pair of gloves on Valentine's Day, he's asking her to marry him. And if she wears them to church on Easter Sunday, that's her way of accepting."

"You want me to wait until Easter to give you my answer?" she asked teasingly.

"No, but I was thinking Easter might be a nice time for a wedding," he said. "I know I've done everything wrong up till now. I'm trying to make it up to you. To woo you proper like you deserve. To sweep you off your feet and kiss you until you can't catch your breath."

"If I can't catch my breath," she teased, "how am I supposed to accept your proposal? How am I supposed to tell you I love you?"

"I'll breathe for you," he said. And lowered his head to claim her mouth as they sealed a vow for their future.

It was much later when they found their way back to the party. Ben knew he was grinning like a mad fool, but he couldn't help himself. He'd finally done something right, something to be proud of. And most important of all he'd made Georgina happy, something he vowed to spend the rest of his life working on.

Blake stood at the grill, where he brandished the barbecue tools he had fashioned with extra-long handles so no one got burnt near the heat. He gave Ben a knowing grin. "I gather things went as planned," he said, as he heaped ribs on the two plates Benjamin passed him.

"Better than planned," Benjamin said.

"So when's the wedding?" Braydon sidled up for a second helping of ribs in time to overhear the last part.

"We're talking about Easter. Provided you boys get off your lazy butts and get our cabin built."

"Another cabin?" Brody groaned as he joined them, but his grin expressed his approval.

As if on cue the twins arrived, followed by Bradley.

Benjamin glanced across the yard to where his love sat with the other wives. Even at this distance, he heard their delighted, girlish squeals. Georgina must be sharing her news.

Bradley gently elbowed him in the ribs. "They've been waiting a long time for this. Seems we all have."

"I think Storm has the wedding dress half-made already," Blake added.

"I thought I retired my suit when Barron got married," Bishop said. But he was grinning as well.

"Wonderful feast, my friends," Percy said, as he joined them near the grill. "And in keeping with such a joyous occasion, I have a small confession to make. And my own gift to contribute to the family." The last was directed to Brody.

"What's that?" Brody asked.

Percy reached into an inside pocket and pulled out a familiar object. Benjamin's jaw dropped as Percy offered them the item, resting it across both palms.

"I wasn't sure who had claim on this, or the proper way to deal with it, so I'll just lay it out here."

It being the knife Hawkes had always worn on his belt after he took it from the twins' brother the night they saw Hawkes kill him.

Brody narrowed his eyes as he faced Percy. "Marshal Philips told me they suspect this to be the murder weapon."

"Afraid that's true," Percy said.

"He also said Hawkes was stabbed seven times."

"Also true," Percy said. "One blow for each of you. I know you all would have liked a go, but my way seemed better. If anyone should wind up in jail for killing that skunk, it's better that it be me."

"You know," Brody said. "Philips suspected someone deliberately tried to implicate us in Hawkes's death."

"Exactly as I hoped," Percy said. "I was more than happy to do what had to be done when I ran across Hawkes on the road the night of the wedding. I knew you were all at the wedding, but in case any suspicion should come your way, I thought an imaginary enemy would be the perfect fall person."

Percy turned to the twins. "Since this belonged to your brother, I couldn't just dispose of it without your blessing. I also don't think any of us wants to be found with it on his person."

Barron and Bishop both reached for the knife at the same time. "We'll bury it next to Joe's body."

"We'll all help," Brody said. "After it gets dark. Bradley, it's your anniversary party. The ladies will have our hides if we don't get over there and pay them some attention. Benjamin, you best get over to Georgina's side and act like a proper doting fiancée before she changes her mind."

Benjamin faced Percy. "I'm not sure if thank you is the appropriate thing to say or not."

Percy nodded. "I understand you all had reason to hate him, but so did I. He was a threat to everyone who matters to me."

Benjamin noticed Percy made no reference to the woman he was still trying to get over.

Blake grabbed the plates from Benjamin's hand. "Georgina won't appreciate cold ribs. Let me get you some hot ones."

Benjamin addressed Percy. "I'm thinking about running for sheriff around here."

"Great idea," Percy said.

Benjamin nodded. "It'll be a relief not having to look over my shoulder for some enemy in the shadows who has it out for me and mine."

Percy nodded. "We'll all count on you to drive away anyone who dares darken our town with evil intent."

"No more treasure hunts in your future?"

"I wouldn't say that, old boy. I still think Henny and I came close to finding de Iturbe's ship of black pearls. I believe it's here someplace, and I aim to find it."

~

Six weeks later...

EASTER MORNING DAWNED as fine and fair a day as any Arizona had seen. Benjamin fell even more in love with Georgina when she suggested the recently repurposed Dove House as her choice for where to hold their wedding. Storm had shown up a couple of weeks ago with the house's first guests, a young woman named Elsie, with her baby.

"So much bad has been associated with that ranch. But it's all in the past. It's time we help erase those memories and let everyone know that, from now on, starting with our wedding day, Dove House will be known as a place of joy and hope for the future."

Brody, in charge of the wedding rings, stood next to Benjamin. Lined up alongside him were the other five brothers. Benjamin tugged on his collar. Getting married was truly a nerve-racking ordeal.

"Who's that couple with the baby that Laura's talking to?" he asked. Today's guest list had been extensive, but the couple were total strangers. Maybe they were friends of Georgina.

"That's Laura's cousin, Robert," Brody said. "They grew up next door to each other in Yuma, but lost touch when Laura and her family moved away. He heard she'd come back to the area and came by and introduce her to his wife. Georgina insisted they stay for the wedding." He patted

Benjamin on the arm. "Not much longer now till the torture is over."

Benjamin had never felt this nervous, not even when he had single-handedly faced a half a dozen armed men. "Did you find it torture, too?"

Brody smiled. "Don't worry. It's all worth it."

GEORGINA HADN'T BEEN able to choose just one of her friends to be matron of honor but insisted all the Mason brides take part in the ceremony. As the wedding march began, played by one of Amanda's music students on the harp, the attendants started the procession led by Lily, the most recent one to be married, and ending with Georgina, who looked positively radiant as she made her way to her intended.

From his seat in the front row, Percy watched the happy couple pledge their troth, expressions serious, unable to take their eyes off each other. He expelled a regretful sigh as he thought of his own unrequited love, his Hope, and the future together that had been denied them both.

Join my VIP Readers Newsletter Group and receive a free copy of PERCY'S HOPE to find out just what Percy got up to when he was away in Colorado. http://eepurl.com/bVosbI

Percy gets a second change to rekindle the flame with his unrequited love in HOPE, Book 1, Widows of the Wild West.

Excerpt from HOPE
Copyright © 2020 Kathleen Lawless

PERCY OPENED the front door of his home to see an agitated-looking Henrietta standing there. "Come in, my dear. What's wrong. Is Braydon—"

"He's fine. The family is fine."

Percy searched her face. "But you're not fine, Henny. Something or someone has clearly ruffled your feathers, which I know to be no easy feat."

As Henrietta preceded him inside, her gaze darted about the place as if seeing it for the first time, before she swung about to face him, her expression troubled.

"Do you remember when we first came to Bullet?"

Percy laughed. "How could I forget? It's only been a few years, but it seems like a lifetime ago."

"Exactly. Who would have thought we'd both end up living here?" Henrietta said. "You overheard that ridiculous bet Braydon made with his brothers regarding me, and you were a good enough friend to let me know what was going on."

"Of course," Percy said, wondering where this trip down memory lane was headed.

"And now I know something I feel you should be privy to. But I'm reluctant to interfere, the way you were then."

"You've started it now," Percy said. "Best to continue."

Henrietta pressed her lips together, clearly torn, before she blurted out, "Hope's in town. She just arrived and plans to stay a few days. She has no idea you're here, and it is possible your paths won't cross. Especially if you were to leave now for the dig site and stay there till after she's gone."

Percy kept his expression neutral. "You said she doesn't know I'm here. What, exactly, *did* she say?"

"I take it you must have mentioned my name to her at some point, because she knew who I was from my hotel name badge. She said she'd heard about the town from you, and had a hankering to see the place for herself."

"Was she alone?"

Henrietta nodded.

"No mention of her husband?"

Henrietta shook her head as her worried gaze met his. "What will you do?"

"What I always do. Pretend life is a game of chess and study the situation carefully before I consider my next move."

"Is there anything I can do to help?" Henrietta asked.

"Not a thing, my sweet."

Want to meet Laura's cousin, Robert, and his mail-order bride? They can be found here in *Mail Order Olivia*.

Excerpt from MAIL ORDER OLIVIA
Copyright © 2020 Kathleen Lawless

ROBERT FULSOM PACED the train platform in Yuma, practicing what he would say to his mail-order bride when she arrived. Sorry for dragging her across the country didn't seem adequate. He had to make sure she realized it was nothing to do with her—it was him. He simply wasn't ready to take on a wife.

He glanced again at the telegram in his hand. Olive Brown. He had no idea what she looked like, but even her name sounded drab, poor thing. He'd heard many of these mail-order brides were either homely or plump, forced to marry a stranger sight-unseen because they had no suitors back east. He had to tactfully ensure she didn't think he was rejecting her because of her appearance.

IN THE CRAMPED TRAIN SEAT, Olivia cradled her sleeping daughter to her chest, grateful for the respite after more than a week of trying to keep Chloe entertained, when all the little bundle of energy wanted to do was crawl around and try to walk. At thirteen months, Olivia expected Chloe would be taking her first step any day.

She deliberately hadn't used her real name in her telegram to Robert. At first, she'd been overjoyed to learn he wasn't dead as she'd been led to believe. Then doubt set in. Why had he not returned for her as promised? And why was his ad for a bride tucked into a coat pocket of her deceased husband?

Get your copy of *Mail Order Olivia* today.

Thanks for reading *Benjamin's Bride*. You might not know how important reader reviews are, but they mean a lot. Just a short sentence saying you enjoyed the book goes a long way with new readers and puts a smile on this author's face.

Review wherever your purchased *Benjamin's Bride* or on Goodreads or BookBub.

And please keep in touch

Website: KathleenLawless.com
Facebook: facebook.com/kathleenlawlessnovels
Instagram: instagram.com/kathleenflawless
TikTok: tiktok.com/@kathleenflawless

If you haven't already done so, sign up for my VIP Reader's Newsletter and be the first to hear about free books, fan-priced sales, and my new series. http://eepurl.com/bVosbI

Dear Reader

The American West in the last half of the nineteenth century offers my heroines a chance to assert their independence and also introduce them to a hero who is their match in every way. My characters have their own ideas of right and wrong, good versus evil, and deal with it on their terms. It wasn't called the Wild West for nothing. Life was about conquest, survival and persistence,

I love writing a historical genre where the reader, by the simple act of picking up the book, instantly suspends disbelief. She easily forgets about her world and her woes in a tale where no one needs to empty the dishwasher or take out the trash, and adventure lies around every corner.

As an author, it's fun to carry her away to a time and place where anything could, and often did, happen. The customs of the day and the manner of dress might be different from today's world, but people are still people. They laugh, love, hurt and heal. Celebrate and mourn. They live life large. And in the untamed wildness of the settling of the west anything can happen.

ALSO BY KATHLEEN LAWLESS

Mail Order Noelle

Chelsea's Choice

Lila: Rescue Me Mail Order Brides

Here Come the Brides Volume 1

Here Come the Brides Volume 2

Sweet Contemporary Romance

Frannie (Always a Bridesmaid)

Baxter (Last Man Standing)

Blue Sky Island

One Cinderella Spring

One Stolen Summer

One Fantasy Fall

One Wondrous Winter

Sweet Christmas Romance Novellas

Holly's Wish

No Groom at the Inn

Steamy Contemporary Romance

SECRET SEDUCTIONS

Her Untamed Cowboy - Book 1

Her Undercover Cowboy - Book 2

Her Unwilling Cowboy - Book 3

Who Needs a Cowboy! - Book 4

Intimate Strangers

Steamy Historical Romance

Taboo

Unmasked

Reckless Rogues - Box Set of the 2 Books

Romantic Suspense

Final Heat

Afterburn

Women's Fiction

Fabulous at Fifty

For a complete book list visit KathleenLawless.com

To be the first to hear about Kathleen's new releases, special fan pricing sales, and also receive a free book, sign up for her VIP Reader Newsletter at http://eepurl.com/bVosb1

ABOUT THE AUTHOR

USA Today Bestselling Author, Kathleen Lawless, blames a misspent youth watching Rawhide, Maverick and Bonanza for her fascination with cowboys, which doesn't stop her from creating a wide variety of interests and occupations for her many alpha male heroes.

With nearly 50 published novels to her credit, she enjoys pushing the boundaries of traditional romance into historical romance, contemporary romance, romantic suspense and women's fiction.

She makes her home in the Pacific Northwest and loves to hear from her readers.

Sign up for Kathleen's VIP Reader Newsletter to receive updates, special giveaways and fan-priced offers. http:// eepurl.com/bVosb1

KathleenLawless.com
Goodreads | BookBub
Facebook | Instagram | TikTok